Luke Warm Saint

by

K. L. Belvin

Luke Warm Saint

Published by
Bravin Publishing, LLC
P.O. Box 340317
Jamaica, New York 11434

ISBN-13: 978 -0-9905377-2-4

Cover by Gregory Graphics, http://www.positiv-media.com
Editing by Maurice M Gray Jr,
http://www.mauricemgrayjr.com
Interior Designed by Bravin Publishing, LLC
www.bravinpublishing.com

Library of Congress Control Number 2015958970

Printed in the United States of America

Luke Warm Saint

DEDICATION

I dedicate this book to my grandmother, Christina Watkins. So much has changed in my life since you were called home, but you shared with me what the Lord told you and it's coming true. Thank you so much for being the conduit for the Lord to help guide me. I am working hard to be the man of God you saw me to be. I love you and miss you daily. Continue to enjoy your time with the Lord.

ACKNOWLEDGEMENTS

First and foremost, I have to acknowledge my Lord and Savior Jesus Christ. Having you in my life has allowed me to be a light to others and I will continue to serve You to the best of my abilities.

I cannot express enough thanks to my loving mother, Katrina Belvin and my father, Elijah Causey;

To Jovan Roseboro, Stephanie C. Harper, Julia Press Simmons, Shonell Bacon, and my dude, Kenneth Wilson for being my professional sounding board at various times with this project.

My completion of this book could not have been accomplished without the support and help of Brian Groves. A life coach who set our talk times, at 3 am his time in Europe, but did so to accommodate me while offering sound advice and compassionate kicks where needed. Thank you for all you've done for me.

To Tammy Harris and Lisa Burton who both kept on top of me for the completion of this book. You guys made sure I was writing when I didn't want to. I appreciate you taking the time to pre-read the book and offering honest feedback.

Finally, to my caring, loving, and supportive wife and daughter, My Queen, Tiffany and my Princess, Kayelle: my deepest gratitude to both of you. Tiffany, your encouragement, when the times got rough, is much appreciated and duly noted. It was a great comfort and relief to know that you were willing to provide assistance while caring for our daughter. I wouldn't be the man I am without you in my life. You are truly a blessing. Thank you Doll. I love you both forever.

Chapter One

"Why do you need so many women?" Kevin muttered. "This is what you spend your money on? Brother, this wasn't how you were raised!"

Kevin stood near the edge of the bed in a room fit for a king and looked into the full-length mirror that sat upon the master dresser. The sound of the shower emanating from the bathroom reminded him that, as usual, he was not alone.

Kevin had mastered the ability to find inconspicuous locations with great décor for his rendezvous with the various women he loved to sneak around town with. His sexual playground was the John F. Kennedy International Airport's hotel strip, and nothing beat today's choice. The Hilton was luxurious enough for his needs and accepted his educator's discount. Without that, he couldn't afford all these escapades with women ranging from coworkers to mothers of his students to bar pickups.

Kevin paced the plush carpet and enjoyed the feeling of it beneath his feet as he wrestled with his conscience. This one bedroom suite had all the conveniences he needed: a kitchen area with a mini refrigerator, a microwave and sink, and a small lounge area with a table set for possibly two or three more guests. He settled into a leather office chair behind the large executive desk and again relished on the carpet...

The shower stopped. Kevin awaited the emergence of one of his longer affairs. Karen walked into Kevin's crosshairs when she became the newest teacher at Canarsie Middle School. She quickly fell for the quick-witted, handsome, and well-dressed brother who made her smile in the administrative meetings. Kevin had a way of making his flirtatious points, professionally of course, while intoxicating whomever he targeted. For over five months, their jobs as teachers kept them teetering on whether or not to end this secret relationship.

Kevin looked up from his memories just as the bathroom door opened and Karen appeared in the steam-filled doorway. Her full-figured silhouette stood naked at the door with only a towel wrapped around her head. Her arms were folded and her legs were spread shoulder-length apart. As she cleared the mist, the look of discontent on her face became clear.

Kevin couldn't suppress a Cheshire cat grin. "Damn, you look sexy, baby. Why are looking at me like that?"

Karen shot him a scornful look. "Are you going to get dressed, or are you just going to sit there watching porn?"

Kevin hadn't noticed the porn movie was playing the whole time he was in discussion with himself. Karen grabbed another towel off the bed to begin drying her legs. Kevin pulled one of the other towels off the bed and flicked it at her while she dried off.

"Kevin, you love to take all the towels out of the bathroom when you shower. You are so selfish."

She walked around to the other side of the bed where her clothes lay in a pile and joined Kevin on the bed.

"Please, sexy, just get dressed, I'm good." Kevin never took his eyes off of mass of intertwined flesh on the TV screen.

"I just get a kick out of watching these movies as you already know. Plus, I'm doing some research to make sure my game is tight. Maybe you and I could work on a few of the things I just saw."

Kevin bit his bottom lip while trying to flirt. Karen looked him up and down while dressing, smiling at the idea of getting back in bed and helping with Kevin's research.

She adjusted her skirt. "I know you enjoy those nasty films, but I don't understand how you can spend two hours rolling around with me, messing up this fantastic hotel room and still want to look at porn. You should be finished."

"First of all, young lady, I am never finished. Second, I had a wonderful time with you this afternoon." He threw a pillow in her direction. "If you didn't have to get back to your husband, we would still be deep into each other."

"Karen, listen, you have another twenty minutes before you have to go. Why don't we try to find something to do?" He grabbed Karen around the waist and ran his hands along her thick hips, hoping to convince her decision. "Get your hands off me, nasty." Karen swung at him playfully. "I have to get back to the school, pick up my bag and get back home and cook for the family."

Kevin rolled his eyes. "Yeah, yeah, yeah, you run and get home to your husband and make sure you give him a big kiss for me."

"Whatever." Karen shook her head as she frowned. "That's not funny. There's no reason to insult my husband." She got up from the bed and began to gather the rest of her things.

"I can't believe you actually question me about insulting your husband. Why do you act like we're not disrespecting him just being here?"

"Boy, don't go there. I don't need to be reminded we are going to hell for what we are doing here."

"Excuse me?" The tone in the room had grown serious. "Just keep it to what it is, woman. Why do you have to bring the Lord into this?" Kevin moved back to the chair, putting distance between him and Karen.

"So wait, let me get this right. You can insult my husband behind everything we're doing each week, and the minute I say we are going to hell because of it, you get bent out of shape? I don't understand." Karen moved over to Kevin and knelt between his legs as she waited for a response.

"Karen, it's hard for me to explain." Kevin lowered his eyes to the floor, away from Karen as he spoke. "I just don't want to be reminded of heaven, hell and all that other religious stuff. We were talking about your husband, weren't we?"

"Kevin, every time we're together, it's wrong in God's eyes."

Kevin clasped his hands and stared at Karen. He didn't like being reminded of how he was violating the values that were instilled when he was younger. He'd had to hide his adult magazines and movies as a teenager. If his mother or his grandmother even thought he might be looking at naked women, they would have dragged him to church for a spiritual intervention. But, with no father to rein him in and the freedom of a latchkey kid to work with, Kevin had all the time he needed to work on his sexual skills and become the ladies' man he fancied himself to be now.

4

When Karen spoke, Kevin could hear his mother and grandmother all over again. Kevin, it seems like every other day you're with a different woman. One day you're going to pay for living your life like this. Hell is filled with men like you. Good men who allowed their choices to cause them to lose their soul. It's happened to this family before.

They always asked when he was going to settle down, why he didn't give in to the Lord and become a member of the church. Kevin always believed his spiritual life was balanced even if he didn't always follow the rules for being a good Christian. He felt the Lord knew what was in his heart, and that was all that mattered.

"Baby, I'm no church boy. I respect the faith, but I don't need to have it shoved down my throat."

Karen stood. "Kevin, did you hear what you just said? You respect the faith? How are you going to respect the faith when you're sleeping with another man's wife?" Karen walked away and began to brush her hair.

"You know what? I don't want to have this conversation." Kevin stood and looked around for his belongings. "Didn't you say you had to get to the school?"

Kevin picked up his socks and shoes. He turned toward Karen and did what he did best; turn the tables. "You sound like a hypocrite. It doesn't bother you to go home to your husband after all we do?"

Karen slammed down the brush and turned to face Kevin. "My husband doesn't care anymore, so why should I? We used to make love often, and now he can't seem to find his way to the bedroom even when requested. When he does, it feels like I'm Ms. Celie from The Color Purple when she and Mister used to get it on. I lay there while he sleepwalks through the lovemaking. Afterwards, he says

"I'm sorry" for his pitiful performance. He claims it's stress from work.

Karen grabbed the brush and went back to work on her hair. . "To answer your question, hell no it doesn't bother me. It doesn't bother me to get mine. I deserve to get off. I work hard and provide a great home. I take care of the kids and keep everything in order. Why shouldn't I be pleased when I want it?"

Karen didn't realize her voice had grown to the point of shouting. The hurt was clear on her face. Kevin got what he wanted. The focus was off of him.

"I'm sorry, baby." Kevin stood behind Karen, kissed her passionately on the side of her head and whispered in her ear, "I didn't mean to make you upset. I'm fighting with myself and only the Lord knows what I'm dealing with inside. Please forgive me for making you feel bad."

"Oh, so it's a fight to be with me, Mister?" Karen playfully smiled as she laid her head back to receive the butterfly kisses.

I got this now, Kevin thought. He planted one final kiss. "No darling, it's not that. I know certain things are wrong, and I know certain things are right. It would take too long for me to get you to understand what I have been feeling these days. Plus, you have to get back to your husband and your kids."

Kevin winked and patted Karen on her behind while guiding her to the door.

"You're right, Kevin. Can I ask you something, baby?" Karen placed her hands on Kevin's face. "I noticed you seem to drift off lately when we're together before and after sex. I'll leave it alone if you want me to. I just hope all is well with us. I enjoy what we have no matter how wrong it is. If I didn't know better, it's like I'm with two different people."

Kevin gave her a bright smile. "There's nothing wrong. I promise."

She kissed his cheek and smiled, but her eyes said she didn't believe him.

"Okay. I'll call you later, handsome."

Kevin opened the door and placed another kiss on Karen's forehead as she headed down the hallway. He peered out of the window to watch Karen walk to her car. As she pulled off, his head turned toward the sunny afternoon sky. He gazed through the big hotel window and released his self-reflecting thoughts about the earlier conversation.

At that moment, the same strong eerie feeling returned. These same feelings had twisted and turned inside him for years. Kevin felt as if his soul was wrestling with itself. His struggles with right and wrong were not new. He believed he could completely turn off the feelings he knew to be wrong and switch back to some sense of normalcy at a moment's notice.

The fear of the consequences of his actions had been drawing closer. He felt like his grandmother stood right next to him and whispered her favorite prediction in his ear.

"One day you're going to preach my funeral."

The feelings engendered by that statement and from spending all those years in church were buried deep inside him, and those feelings would not be silenced. After thirty minutes of this personal tug of war, Kevin decided to check out. He slipped on his Ray Ban sunglasses and walked over to his 2013 Dodge Durango. Kevin liked stylish things since they attracted the ladies, yet he wouldn't throw away money if he could avoid it.

After putting his seatbelt on, he picked up his cell phone and dialed Karen's number. The feeling he had earlier returned. A little voice spoke to him, saying, "Stop messing around with another man's wife."

He drowned the voice out by thinking of what he had done with Karen that afternoon.

"Did you reach the school yet, sexy?" Kevin asked.

"Yes, baby, I'm already on my way home. Why, you thinking about Big Mama?" Kevin could feel her smile.

"Hold on a second, Sexy. I need to put my Bluetooth in before I get stopped by the police. You know NYPD is popping folks for using their cell phones behind the wheel these days"

He got his headset on without losing the call. "Karen, listen, I'm not coming in tomorrow but I'll give you a call in the morning. What time are you coming to work?"

"I start at 8:35 on Thursdays, but I'll get there at 7:30. My husband drops me off on Thursdays. I leave my baby at home since there is never anywhere to park on Tuesdays and Thursdays"

"Oh OK, cool. I already called Mr. Jackson and left a message for him, that I won't be in tomorrow."

Karen let out a loud sigh. "Do you have incriminating pictures on that man? I don't have any idea how he is so mean to every other person in the school except you. If I didn't know better, I would think you two…"

Karen paused as Kevin grunted into the phone at her insinuation.

His face turned to stone. "Don't you even think about finishing that thought. You know there isn't anything homosexual about me."

"Okay baby, relax I was just joking."

Kevin nodded and kept quiet. Karen didn't need to know that it wasn't Mr. Jackson he had in his back pocket, but the principal Ms. Jose. Kevin had slept with parents, fellow teachers and other members of the school staff when he thought he could get away with it, but his first conquest at Canarsie was the principal herself. Ms. Jose was 55, looked 35 and loved men who were as young as she looked.

There had always been talk Kevin secured his position by being "Ms. Cougar's boy toy." Kevin felt he got the job on his own merits, but didn't object to being called to the principal's office for "long lunch dates."

Karen kept talking, but Kevin's mind was with Ms. Jose during their last intimate encounter. She often called for Kevin to come to her office for "mentoring," which pretty much the whole school knew was him filling the role of her personal sexual maintenance man. By day, Kevin Watkins was a nurturing role model at IS 211 Intermediate School, who lived to service the educational needs of his students and the needs of the school. The rest of the time he was a sexual monster whose explosive appetite kept him constantly on the prowl.

"Kevin, are you listening to me?"

Kevin snapped out of his reverie and focused back on the road and on his conversation with Karen. "I got you. I am hearing everything you're saying, Sexy.

As Kevin listened to Karen explain her conspiracy theory, his phone beeped.

"Hold on a second, Baby." Kevin clicked over. "Hello? Richard!"

"What's up, my brother? How are you?"

Kevin laughed. I was getting some food. I went out for an early dinner. Can I hit you back in about ten minutes?"

Richard laughed. Let me guess. You're at some sleazy hotel."

"No sir. I'm not at the hotel. I just left." Kevin snickered. "Brother, can I please call you back?" Kevin pushed the talk button again. "I'm back, Karen. It was Richard."

"Did you tell him about us? I know you tell your best friends everything, don't you?"

Kevin smiled coyly. "Nope, not everything." Kevin held up two crossed fingers as he responded to her query. "OK, maybe I do tell them a few things but not every little detail."

"Do they know about me being married?"

"Karen, everyone in Canarsie knows you're married. Canarsie is not that small, but people talk. Why do you think we drive way out here to Queens to come to the hotel?"

"How long have you and your boys been friends?"

Kevin frowned at the question since he was trying to get off the phone and didn't want to discuss his friends. He knew describing his friends was like describing the turmoil going on inside him. However, he offered Karen an answer.

"Richard and I grew up together on the same block here in Brooklyn, and James moved into the neighborhood from Delaware when we were 10."

Canarsie sat right off the Belt Parkway in Brooklyn. It was in an area that many did not come to unless it was for a particular purpose. Most drove through Canarsie and its middle class homes on their way to other areas of Brooklyn.

"Oh OK, now it makes sense why you three are as thick as thieves."

"I wouldn't say thieves Sexy, ever since Richard found the Lord, he's been a different man. I couldn't be happier for him. Watching him reminds me there's a place for me at the Lord's Table."

Kevin smiled as he remained focused on the road.

"I haven't gotten to where he is yet. I could one day see myself preaching if I ever allowed the Lord to take his place in my life." He chuckled at himself. "I know my time is coming to join the church. Just not sure when I am going to give up this life I have."

Karen laughed so hard Kevin had to remove his earpiece until she finished. "Yeah right, Kevin. If the Lord saves you, then there's hope for anybody."

Kevin frowned. "Ouch, that hurts, Karen."

"Come on, Kevin, stop playing. You becoming a man of God? I would leave my husband if that ever happened."

Karen's tone changed to one of confidence, knowing the chances of her having to leave her husband wouldn't happen.

"That really hurt, baby. You just bought yourself a spanking when I see you." Kevin ended his words in a playful tone.

Karen matched Kevin's playful tone. "You better not leave a mark on me. My crazy husband would kill me and come looking for you."

Kevin smirked. "Ahh, don't worry. I'm not scared. Tell him that you slipped and fell."

"Yeah, with a palm print on my behind?"

"Let me get off this phone, doll. I'll call you tomorrow after school."

"Bye, baby." Karen whispered before hanging up.

After enjoying the 25-minute ride to his home, Kevin pulled up to his condo. He liked the ranch style look to his apartment. It reminded him of the small home where he grew up. His apartment showed off his many educational awards, and an immaculate décor that made people think a woman lived there.

The furniture was made of Italian leather and was fashioned with heavy stitching. It was designed to look expensive but made to last for a long time. Kevin refused to waste money. As he fell back onto the couch and put his feet up, he picked up his new iPhone. He kept that as his lifeline to the outside world, especially the many women who occupied his life.

Kevin kept his promise from earlier. "Richard, my man. What's the deal, sir?"

"I'm good, Kevin, how are you?"

"Ahhhh, I'm tired. Like I said, I had a late dinner."

"Yeah, right. What was her name this time? You probably were with Karen."

"Damn! Am I that predictable?"

"Yes, sir, you are. You have been that way since we were children. How do you think I knew how to keep you out of trouble?"

"Listen, Richard, I'm having a ball living my life. We've only been at this for about four or five months. It's been pretty cool. I really like her."

"Kevin, are you crazy? She's married, Dawg. I mean, you're blatantly throwing your business in the Lord's face. At some point, He's going to answer back and you're not going to like it when it happens."

Kevin's lips tightened; he fought to keep anger out of his voice. "Richard, please don't preach to me tonight. Brother, I love you, and I know you have my back, but please let me figure this out on my own. You are starting to sound like my grandmother. Can we just have one conversation and you not bring the Lord into it?"

"I'm sorry, Brother, I know you would like me to step to the side and act like sinning is okay. It's not. And Brother, you have so much going on for you. Why would you want to thumb your nose at the Lord?"

Richard dug in, knowing he was one of the few who had Kevin's ear when it came to his behavior. "I am sure it has to bother you to know you're not living your life correctly. Do you know what good you could do as an educator and man of God teaching folks the Word?"

Kevin's eyes widened, shocked that Richard read his inner feelings through the phone. Despite it, he wouldn't tip his hand to what had been going on inside him lately. He knew Richard would latch on like a pit bull if he spoke on the feelings of guilt or whatever the eerie feelings were he had been having.

"Richard, I am not thumbing my nose at the Lord. You as much as anyone knows that I don't want to be disrespectful to the Lord. I'm just a single man trying to enjoy my life. I understand who the Lord is. I respect the Lord. I'm just doing me." Kevin sounded like a used car salesman trying to convince his friend.

"What?" Richard's voice echoed loudly through the phone. Kevin moved the phone away from his ear from the level of disgust in Richard's voice. "Kevin, how many times are we going to have this conversation? You can't respect the Lord if you're going to turn around and act totally opposite what His Word says. You know what's in the Bible better than I do. We don't have to talk about this, but you say things that drive me crazy."

Richard loved Kevin, but his tone cut deep since they were closer than any two friends or brothers could be. "You and I have shared the same Bible Study class and even got baptized on the same day, or at least I was." Sadness echoed in Richard's voice. "Even with all you've learned, I don't understand how you can do exactly what's opposite."

Richard stayed on Kevin harshly because he knew returning to the church and the Lord was what saved his life. He truly believed inside Kevin was something special. He had stood up for him when many others had nothing else to say but negative comments. He also knew Kevin was a master liar after being with so many women over the years. Richard had dedicated his life to saving the lives of his friends.

"Kevin, your mother and grandmother raised you in the church as did mine. How come it's never taken hold? We ran the streets. We lived like whores and thugs. But there comes a time to give in and let the Lord have his way before it's too late. You seem to have this fight going on inside you, and you're playing both sides of the fence. I can see it, Brother."

Kevin remained silent. "You can't be lukewarm for the Lord, Brother!" Richard took a moment to sigh; his pain could be heard in his passion for his friend's salvation.

Kevin sighed. Brother, don't get upset and don't give up on me. Your words have taken hold." Kevin stood and walked to his kitchen, needing to clear his head as he spoke. "It's just that I see it differently. I mean, I'm glad you got saved. I'm glad that when the Lord spoke, you decided running in these streets wasn't for you anymore. I understand that. When you found Chelle and started making babies, no one was happier than me."

Kevin stood at the doorway of the kitchen and lowered his head. "Listen, Richard, I'm stoked for you, Brother.

Looking at you and the changes you've made, I know there's hope for me. However, Brother, it has to be in my own time. I mean, come on. Think about it. God doesn't want you to force me to come to him. If you force anyone to find the Lord, it would make His words false. Partner, God doesn't want me to come to him by force. He wants me to come on my own with the free will he gave all of us."

Richard felt a rush as Kevin reached into that spiritual place inside him. "Yes, Kevin, I see you still have the teaching inside you. You spoke the truth, and now you can stop with the manipulation game you're playing. It's not going to work. I'm not one of your women, and you're gonna hear me out You and I both know no one knows how many days they have on this planet. Do you want to die and have to face God with all the foolishness you've been a part of?"

With a pause, Kevin took a moment to look around the living room and then to the ceiling. He inhaled. "Richard, you want the truth? This is going to sound real crazy. I honestly believe that God is not going to kill me anytime soon." The eerie feelings resurfaced as each word crossed his lips. Kevin ignored them, but this time they were constant and throbbing. With each word, he could feel something poking at his soul.

"Don't say that, Kevin! You know the term from your lips to God's ears?"

Kevin stood firm on his words. "Yes, I do. Very well."

Richard's voice boomed through the phone. "Well, understand you may be signing your own death warrant."

"OK, see now I have to go, man. You're jumping off the deep end of the pool with this one."

"No, no, no, hear me out, Kevin, please."

"No, Richard, you hear me out. I'm being serious right now." With each word, the feeling grasped Kevin and a look of confusion and fear took over. Yet he still resisted, not knowing what it could be.

Kevin's humble tone was evident with each word. "Richard, I pick my Bible up every now and then and read it when I am here in the house. When I do, I get a feeling that I have a connection to the Lord. I just don't believe that right now where I'm at is where He wants me to be for what He wants me to do, and when the time comes, I'll know it."

"Kevin, I understand all you're saying. However, we both know everyone has to pay for their sins at some point in their life. You will pay for yours, and it won't be pretty."

"Yeah, I'm sure I will, but I'll be able to deal with it when the time comes. So far, whatever the Lord's laid out in front of me, I've been able to deal with."

"Kevin, are listening to what you've just said? I love you. You are my brother, but you have to become more fearful of the Lord. You have to get closer to the Lord and say "I am sorry." You have to change before it's too late. The Lord will have the final say in this dangerous game you're playing."

Richard decided to let Kevin off the hook for now. "Hey partner, let me get off this phone. I was going to stop by anyway. Are you going to be home for a little while?"

Relief washed over Kevin at the end of this discussion. "Yes, I am." Oh, Richard, listen, pick up some beer. We haven't shared a drink in a little while."

"Kevin, you know I don't drink anymore."

"Now you know Jesus had a sip of wine, so let's share this beer like we used to."

"I'll think about it, partner."
"Listen, pick it up and we will talk when you get here."

K. L. Belvin

Chapter Two

Karen hung up from Kevin. She stopped at the gas station to put gas into her car. She noticed two young men looking at her new car and of course they took a look at her shapely legs as she pumped her gas. Karen's husband, Thomas, gave her the 2013 blue and silver trimmed Mini Cooper, and it quickly became her favorite possession... She hooked up her Bluetooth, placed a call and put the phone in its holder before sliding behind the wheel.

"Hello, baby. How was your meeting today?"

Karen smiled. "Hey, baby. You know how things are with these meetings. Boring and not much to learn but they make us go anyway."

She adjusted her hair in the mirror, determined to get herself together before heading home.

"Listen Thomas, I'm on my way home. Do you want something to eat?"

"No I just want to see my wife."

Karen disconnected the call and pulled out of the gas station to head home. She pulled into her driveway twenty minutes later to find Thomas waiting at the front door.

"Hey baby. Glad you're home."

Karen frowned as she approached the front door. "Is there a reason you also have to come out of the house to watch me get out of my car?"

Thomas reached out to touch Karen's hair as she drew near.

"Your hair feels wet."

"Why do we have to do this every time I get home? You know I love you and wouldn't cheat on you. Now come in the house and stop this foolishness."

19

Thomas turned to the side to allow Karen to pass and chuckled.

"Listen woman, you know I'm crazy about you. I don't know what I would do if I found out you cheated on me. I just love what we have and I don't want to lose this."

Karen stopped walking as Thomas moved in close behind her and put his hands on her shoulders. She relaxed into his touch, and he wrapped his arms around her.

"Baby I see other guys whose wives lay next to them every day and the whole time living a different life. I couldn't handle anything like that with us. I know we have our problems, but I love you to death. Kevin placed a kiss on the back of Karen's head while inhaling her scent.

Karen sighed and gently disengaged from his rebuke disguised as extreme affection. She tossed her school bag and pocketbook onto the couch and turned to Thomas.

"Baby listen I have a tough enough job trying to teach my students. I don't have the time or energy to carry on with another man. I love you and this is where I want to be."

Karen had lots of practice lying to Thomas. Over their ten years of marriage, she'd learned just how jealous he can be. It wasn't easy to fool him, but Kevin was worth it to her. She had to constantly think of new ways to see him without getting caught.

As Karen headed into the kitchen, Thomas quietly slid over to the couch. Thomas prayed he wouldn't find anything incriminating in Karen's things.

Karen came out faster than expected. Thomas backed away from her belongings and tried not to bring attention to himself. Unfortunately, he forgot to put Karen's cell phone back into her bag and Karen noticed right away.

"Seriously? Thomas, you're still checking my phone. Didn't we talk about this before? You agreed to stop this mess."

Thomas blushed. "Listen I can't help myself. I told you that. I don't want to check, but at times I feel like you are drifting away from me. Then I see your phone and you still have a code on there. Like you're hiding things from me."

Karen placed her phone back into her bag and walked over to her husband.

"Thomas I told you why. I lock my phone from my students so if they get to my phone, they can't do anything with it. And you know how you are. Like the time I took the picture in my classroom with my colleague and you went ballistic for no reason. What am I supposed to do when no matter what I say to you, it becomes an issue if it doesn't line up quite right with your thinking?"

Thomas slammed his fist into an open palm.

"Karen listen. We don't hang out like we used to and we definitely don't make love all that often. You work all these extra hours and go to all these meetings after school. What am I supposed to think?"

Thomas plopped down hard in his recliner.

"You must think I'm stupid. I know something is wrong with us. I just have this sick feeling you're cheating on me."

Karen looked her husband in the eye and put on her best "game face." Given Thomas' jealousy, she had to perfect a look that showed no worry or guilt whenever she dealt with it.

"Listen baby, you know I love only you. You also know how much work teaching is. I went to the same amount of meetings last year and the year before that. Every time I'm around a man, you get worried or act a fool.

If I were cheating on you, where would I find the time and still get my work done? When you call, I'm there. When you text me, I hit you right back. I don't go out with my girlfriends as much and when I'm coming or going, I call you."

Karen walked back toward Thomas. She knelt at his feet, put her hands on his thighs and looked up into his face.

"Baby you know I love you and we made love last week. Don't tell me you forgot about Friday night. It was great. It was great right?"

Thomas exhaled and leaned back.

"Baby I'm sorry. You just know how I feel about you. The idea of you with another man drives me crazy. I really don't know what I would do if I found out you were lying all this time. But you're right. When I call, you're there. You do hit me back and I know you do a lot for those children."

Thomas leaned forward, lifted Karen's hand to his lips and kissed her palm.

"You just make sure you're telling me the truth. I swear you better be telling me the truth."

Karen stood and released a loud breath as she walked away. Thomas watched her go and reached for the remote, talking to himself the whole time.

"She thinks I'm so stupid. I'll catch her behind one of these days. Just watch. She better not be out with anyone. She thinks I'm so stupid."

Thomas nodded his head as if agreeing with himself. He leaned back in the chair and kept switching channels.

Chapter Three

Hours later, Richard hopped in his car to head over to Kevin's house. His 2009 Dodge Caravan was the prototypical family van, far removed from the fancy cars he used to drive when he was a drug dealer. Instead of living a pulse-pounding life full of danger and women, he now thrived on being married with two children and active in his church. He was grateful to be alive after all the things he did in life.

For the 25-minute drive from Long Island to Kevin's place, Richard put in a mix music CD of many of his favorite gospel recording artists. He fast forwarded to Yolanda Adams' "This Battle Is Not Yours," a song that had gotten him through many a tough situation.

Driving along the dark highway, Richard turned the music down to share a moment in prayer. "Heavenly Father, I ask that You protect Kevin from himself. Grant me the insight to help Kevin understand what he is doing is wrong. Father, You saved me from death from my sins. I ask that You grant me a way to reach Kevin in any way you see fit. I ask that You protect him while I work on his soul down here. I am sure You are working on him from the inside.

"Heavenly Father, even if it costs me my life, I won't stop working on his soul. I ask you to show me the way to do your will. I ask this in Jesus' name. Amen."

Richard wiped the tears that fell during his prayer and pulled up in front of Kevin's house. As he reached Kevin's door, his thoughts returned to his friend. Richard knew

Kevin always wanted an apartment like the ones he saw on TV, and this was it. He remembered Kevin looking so hard for the design that fit his modern and homey taste.

Richard stopped a few feet away from the door of Kevin's condo. *I say one thing for Kevin,* he thought. *He can afford this on a teacher's salary because he's been careful enough not to become a baby daddy. Not easy to do with all the women he has.*

Richard rang the doorbell and prepared himself to finish the earlier conversation.

"Richard, hey buddy." Kevin greeted his friend with a big smile and hug. "Come in, man, and have a seat. How are we doing tonight, T. D. Jakes?"

"That is not funny, Kevin. It really isn't. You play too much, Brother."

Kevin smiled. "OK, man, you are way too uptight, Richard. You take being a man of God to serious. But you know I love you, my dude. I guess before it's all said and done, I might end up preaching."

Richard couldn't return the smile. "Listen, Kevin, we need to finish our earlier conversation. Please have a seat and listen to me."

Kevin frowned. "Brother, you are not going to come into my home and tell me what to do."

Richard shot back a thunderous response. "Kevin, I've listened to all of your BS for years. May I have the damn floor?"

Richard lifted his gaze to the ceiling and shook his head. "You know I was nowhere near spiritual when I was hustling. I thought I was on top of the world. I had money. I had women doing whatever I asked. I thought I had it all, yet, I was so unhappy I felt like I was dying."

Kevin rubbed his hands and smiled as his thoughts faded to the past.

"Yes, Richard, I remember those days. You were doing your thing. When you were on top of the drug game, I think I was having sex twice a day off your leftovers."

Richard took a seat as he spoke. "What seemed like fun didn't matter. I wasn't happy. Then all of a sudden, the Lord touched me, and it was as if a weight had been lifted from my chest, from my life."

"Yeah, I remember. You became a whole different person. I thought you were crazy or high to tell you the truth."

Kevin walked over to the same side of the living room where Robert was sitting. "When you first mentioned what was going on with you, you came running through the door talking about the Lord took all your money, freed you from the women, took away the drugs and everything like that. I was like did my brother lose his damn mind?"

Richard's face was stern as he looked toward Kevin for acceptance.

"Kevin, do you understand ten years ago I had a kilo of drugs on the streets? I had money stacked up at various locations around the city. Do you know how hard it was to turn all that in?"

"Yeah, I know, partner. I still don't understand that part. If you just left the drugs on the street, why would you turn the money over to the police? You could have been arrested for that. I think they're still shocked that you walked in and turned in $100,000. What the hell was wrong with you? You're really lucky your crew didn't decided to do an "American Me" move on you. Especially with the thugged out Negros you rolled with"

"Kev, it was received by ill and evil means. It had to be turned in. I told them to do whatever they wanted to do with it and me."

Kevin smirked. "You know they kept that money, don't you?"

"It's not my concern, my brother. They have to deal with the Lord on that one."

"Man, I love you dearly, but you're a stupid dude. You could have been set up for life if you had done things just a little different. God would have understood. Plus you would have put that money to good use." Kevin said, while shaking his head from side to side.

Richard touched the cross he wore around his neck. "Kevin, your focus is all wrong. I'm not stupid at all, my man. You really don't understand what it means to submit to the Lord and give in to His will."

"Yes sir. I'm sorry for calling you stupid." One of these days I'll figure it out."

Kevin's eyes darted from ceiling to floor "Listen, can we talk about something else. What do you and Chelle have planned for this weekend?"

Richard stood and walked toward Kevin. "I have some church business I have to take care of Saturday morning, and then I think I'm going to take everyone to the park and we're going to have lunch there. Why don't you stop by? The kids need to see their uncle."

Kevin smiled. "True. Anthony and Kierra are my favorite little rug rats."

"What do you mean your favorites? They're your only niece and nephew."

"True."

"You better enjoy them. You know James isn't having any kids any time soon."

Kevin laughed, thinking of his other childhood friend. "Don't speak too soon, Richard. James might have a couple kids he's not claiming."

Richard placed his hands on Kevin's shoulders, shaking his head. "Oh Lord I hope not. Now that I think about it, I have to hit James up. I haven't talked to him in a few days. You know he doesn't vibe with me as much these days."

James and Richard had drifted slowly apart since Richard's commitment to his faith. Kevin seemed to serve as the conduit between both of them in their older years.

"Well, you know the deeper you got into church, James felt he had to distance himself. In my opinion, Richard, it's because I don't think he wants to bring any negative vibes toward you and your family. Especially owning the type of club he does. So, he tries to stay away."

"Yes, I know, but I look past what he does for a living because we are friends. As a man of God, I have tried to talk him out of it many times. I pray for him often these days. He is still our boy, Kevin. I know James has a good heart, I just don't understand how he can own such a spot and allow all those men to toss their money and their lives away?"

Richard paced the floor. This conversation about James was not easy on him. He constantly asked himself how was he to keep a friendship with a man who lived completely opposite what he w morally.

Kevin leaned forward, concern etched across his face. "How can you say you don't understand? Listen, he did you a favor. He moved the club to Long Island so it wouldn't come back to haunt our friendship. Plus, he's making pretty good money at it, and it's legal, Bro. It's a legal business, so it's not like he's hustling as you used to do."

"Kevin, he's selling sex, and it's so opposite what the Word says. He is going to pay for what he's doing. I am trying hard to save him as I was saved."

Emotions swelled up in Richard's face. His love for James went without question. But he was in a fight, the Lord or his friendship.

"I know James doesn't care to know the Lord as I do, but I'm going to keep trying to save his soul. I was out there and don't want to see my friend go to hell over money and sex."

Richard clenched his fist and teeth while speaking. Richard was often torn at times dealing with his friends' choices in life. He fought not to judge them for he knew they were great guys at heart, but where was the line in the sand when you say you love the Lord?

Kevin stood and rolled his eyes. "Here you go. Everything is about the Bible and you being saved. Richard, please, men are going to get laid. Men are going to pay for it, and they are paying James by the bundle. I don't see anything wrong with that. He is not forcing men to sin. I have seen some of the women that he has there, and I love it! I go there myself once or twice every couple of weeks. He has a couple of girls that are only for the VIP folks, and let me tell you..."

Richard shook his head. "Please, Kevin, I don't want to hear the rest."

"OK, married man. I'll spare you the sexy details. It would take me about 20 to 25 minutes to explain what they can do to a man. There's some nastiness going on over there, and I love it!" Kevin smiled as if he had just won the lottery.

"Kevin, you're going to be the death of me. I told the Lord even if it kills me, I am going to get you to understand the Lord is watching everything and you need to change your ways."

Kevin's expression changed as Richard's last statement reached his soul. Richard knew Kevin didn't like to hear things like that, having lost his grandfather and several students to senseless violence.

"Richard, please, I don't want to hear it anymore."

Kevin and Richard both moved to the door. Richard knew when to leave well enough alone. Any mention of violence tended to pull the scab off soft wounds. Kevin loved his grandfather, who was the closest thing to a father Kevin had. In turn, Kevin was the father figure to many of his students. Each loss cut just as deep as the ones before it. Teaching in Brooklyn, he tried as hard as he could to deal with the problems in the streets.

"OK, church boy, you win for now. I have to hit James up to see what he is doing."

Richard, knowing Kevin was trying to bring the night to a positive close, asked, "If you talk to him before I do, tell him to give me a call." As Richard walked out the door, Kevin's face changed, going from a smile to a somber expression.

"Richard."

"Yes, Kevin?"

"Listen, man, don't give up on me. I may not say it often, but I love the fact you try so hard to get James and me to see the Godly light. I know the Lord is real, but I have to get there on my own."

Richard nodded and smiled as he headed toward his car. "Kevin, it's really simple. The Lord doesn't like a person who is lukewarm. Either be on fire for Him or leave it alone. The in-between person does more damage. You are going to call down the anger of the Lord, and He will make you see things the way they should be. You know this better than I do, and you should be teaching it to others."

"Man, get out of my face with that gloom and doom mess. Call me later, Rich." Kevin waved and turned to head back into the house.

To avoid thinking about everything Richard said, Kevin looked around and decided to focus on cleaning. "Hmm, it's been a minute. I need to clean this house. Look at this place. No chick is going to want to hang out here. Let me see when the housekeeper is scheduled to be here." He wandered through the living room to the kitchen to look at the calendar he kept on the refrigerator. "OK, I have the housekeeper coming Saturday. That'll work perfectly. The housekeeper can come, and I'll hang out at the park with my niece and nephew. I hope they send an ugly chick because that sexy number they sent two weeks ago had me going."

Chuckling, he added, "I tried to get her phone number but she was married and faithful ... so she said. I don't understand these chicks. I just wanted to go around the block a couple of times. I wasn't trying to get her to leave her husband."

Falling upon his couch, Kevin shook his head and ran a hand over his face. "Let me call my mother. I haven't talked to her in a few days." Lying back on the couch, Kevin picked up his cell phone. Kevin was excited to hear his mother's voice.

After the second ring, Kevin's mother picked up. "Hey, Ma."

Sounding as excited as her son, she responded, "Hey, Baby. What's going on? So, you remember the old woman who gave birth to you."

"Mom, come on. You know I've been busy. How are you doing?"

"I'm doing good, son. I'm hanging in there."

"Sounds great, lady." Kevin became a little boy when talking to his mother. She and his grandmother were the center of his world. He loved them to no end.

Sounding like Florida Evans from Good Times, Kevin's mother said, "Well, Casanova, you finally decided to call your old mother. You found time between your conquests to think about me, wow."

"Aw, stop, Mom. I just saw you at church on Sunday."

"Very true, son, but when was the last time you stopped by?" Kevin had been the man in her life. She loved him but understood a man of his age was not going to sit around his mother too often. It didn't stop her from missing her son.

"It was Sunday, Ma, after church," Kevin said, trying to convince his mother of his seriousness.

"Well then, lover man, let me ask you this… when are you going to stop spending your time in church looking at the women and actually listen to what the pastor talks about? Even better, when are you going to take the pastor's place and show the gifts the Lord has given you?"

"Please, Ma, I don't want to hear it. The pastor seems to talk about the same things every service."

"Kevin, you don't see that's the Lord speaking to you, not the pastor?"

"Oh, Ma, I didn't call you for this, lady. Let's not start this now. Please?"

Kevin placed his hands over his face. Kevin's mother knew what her son was like, and every chance she got, she tried to get him to give up the life he clung to for one of a spiritual nature.

"No, Kevin, I'm going to start. You're 34. You have a Master's degree, a nice job, a nice apartment. You've got some good friends.... well one good friend. The other one needs to be in church himself. However, James, as nasty as he is with that nasty business he owns, is a good guy where you're concerned. Boy, when are you going to find your way home to the Lord and preach His word?"

Kevin, hearing the tone in his mother's voice, knew where she was going to take the conversation. Every time she spoke about church, she brought up Richard. Kevin tried to find a way out of the same conversation he had with Richard just a few moments earlier. Looking up at the ceiling and shaking he head, he put his plan into motion.

"Don't say it, Mom."

"Yes, I'm going to say it. When are you going to find your way home to the Lord, like Richard? You know you are going to preach the Word whether you want to or not."

Kevin wanted to hang up the phone, but he would never disrespect his mother. He had heard this story for years about him being destined to preach because of a vow his mother made with God when she was pregnant with him. She reminded him about Richard nonstop ever since Richard became saved. It burned at him inwardly, but he had kept it to himself. However, this time his mother got under his skin because with each word, those odd feelings returned.

"Richard was just like you when you two were coming up. He was doing all the things that you were doing. I've heard him speak often at the church about how he was unhappy, so I know you can't be happy with the life you're living."

"Mom, I'm happy with where I am." Kevin ground his teeth as he spoke, trying to hold in what he was feeling about the conversation. He was fighting two battles, one with his mother and one with his inner feelings.

"Say what you want, a mother knows better. A mother knows her son. I know you're not happy, boy, I can feel it in my spirit."

Kevin's plan to sweet talk his mother never got off the ground. Each time he wanted to change the subject, she bore down on him even harder. She loved her son, but it was her fear that kept her talking.

"Ma, listen to me. I don't want to continue this. I read the Word. I understand the Word. I just had this conversation with Richard." Kevin's voice grew louder. "I know what the Lord wants from me. Well, actually, I take that back. I don't know what the Lord wants from me, so I'm just living my life until the Lord decides to let me know where He wants me to go. Sometimes, I wish Richard had never gotten saved. I just think my life would be so much better if he wasn't in the damn church!"

"Boy, you watch your mouth! You better be careful what you ask for! If Richard was not in church, who would lead you back to Christ?"

Kevin softened his tone. "Mom, I am sorry for yelling. Please forgive me,"

"It's OK, boy, it's just the devil trying to hold his place in your life. What he doesn't know is you're going to be a preacher. I don't care what you think or feel about it, you are going to preach the word. It might be over my funeral, but you will preach soon. I claimed it, and I know the Lord has heard my wishes."

Knowing his mother would go on for what seems like forever, like she had in the past, Kevin knew it was time to end this call. "Ma, please stop. You keep talking about this preacher thing. First of all, nobody wants me to be their preacher, all right? Nobody would believe me if I was to stand there and preach." Kevin truly believed what he was saying to his mother. He truly didn't believe preaching was something he would do.

"My son, you are so lost sometimes. You're an educator, but it scares me with what you don't know. Child, you said you read the Bible, right?"

"Yeah, Mom, I do."

"OK, so do you understand that some of the nastiest and negative guys in this world were the guys the Lord used to get out his message to everyone?" Kevin didn't study the Bible like his mother who lived her life by its words. She had grown to trust the Lord with everything. She gave her son over to the Lord years ago, and felt it was her duty to keep him on track so the Lord could use him when the time was right.

"Like who, Ma? Who did the Lord use that even came close to what I do in my life?"

He could feel his mother's smile over the phone. He knew she had one this time; her plan to get him into a conversation about God had worked.

"Well first look at David. King David was on top of the world but wanted some tail from another man's wife and so he lay with her. Now tell me that's not the same as what you're out here doing."

34

When Kevin didn't respond, she continued. "David told lies, lay with another man's wife, and got her pregnant. He then had her husband killed when he couldn't trick him to go home to sleep with her to cover the fact he had already slept with her. God didn't kill him but he paid for it with his own children's lives. Son, the Lord blessed him, but the sins still had to be paid for."

"Ma, please, I have to go." Kevin tried to interject. But his mother was like a pit bull locked in on another animal. She refused to let him off the hook. He asked for this, and she was going to have her say.

"Look at Paul. He was a murderer. When the Lord called on him, his name was changed and he went on to do great things. He wrote most of the New Testament."

With each word, the uneasiness took hold of Kevin. He began to feel like a teenager all over again.

"The Lord has a plan for you, son. This I know. My worry is at what cost and to whom. If not, you just have to find your way. You have to stop being a lukewarm saint."

"Lukewarm saint?" Kevin asked with confusion in his voice. "What the hell does that mean? Richard said the same thing to me, Ma."

"It's easy, son. Everybody around you can see that you have some type of gift when you speak. I've been telling you this since you were a baby. When you open your mouth, when you do the things you do in the classroom, you're phenomenal. When you're focused on whatever you're doing, people respond to you. Are you listening, boy?"

"Yes, Ma, I am."

"Somehow you have this switch you just turn off and on so you can become something different depending on who you're with. Inside you is a soul of a saint, and the

35

Lord made you this way, yet you remain lukewarm about serving him. You love the Lord some days and some days you don't."

"Wait. Ma, what do you mean 'love the Lord some days?' "

"Son, when you openly sin, you are thumbing your nose at the Lord. Hence you're turning your back to the Lord."

"Ok I get it. Now you're really starting to sound like Richard."

"I sound like Richard because he can see what everyone else sees in you. Son, I pray for you every night. I ask the Lord to reach down and touch your soul to somehow make you whole because you're not. You and the devil are dancing this dance, and you keep playing and the Lord is going to smite you, my son. It's going to hurt in such a way that you're really not going to be the same person because of it. The only way the Lord is going to reach you is through some painful situation."

Kevin's mother's voice trembled as she tried to pierce the shell Kevin kept around himself.

"Oh, Ma, would you stop putting the voodoo on me? It's almost like you want the Lord to do something negative to me."

"Son, I can't do anything or make the Lord do anything. He's going to do what he does. Just know I am praying for you. Have you called your grandmother?"

"No, I have not. I'll call her later. Is she downstairs?"

"I think she is. She was lying down earlier, but you should give her a call. She wasn't feeling too well."

Kevin's mother and grandmother shared a two-family home. It gave them the false belief they lived on their own but kept them close enough to be there for each other. Kevin loved the idea because he could see both of them when he came over.

"Do you know if she's up?"

"I don't know. I haven't been downstairs to check on her."

"I'll call later. I'm going to come by tomorrow and just check you two out before the weekend starts."

"All right, baby. Don't forget. I love you."

"I love you, too, Ma."

Kevin was elated to get off the phone. He stared at the high-priced piece of electronics as if it had answers for him.

Kevin needed a reprieve from spiritual matters and decided to check on James. He needed someone who wasn't going to drive him crazy about God, church, or preaching. Quickly, he hopped into his ride and headed to the club.

He couldn't get the conversation with his mother out of his mind. "Lord, that old lady can talk. I thought she was never going to let me get off the phone."

Just as he grabbed his phone to call James, Kevin's phone rang. He smiled. "He must've known I was thinking of him."

"James! What's the deal, dog? I was calling you."

James was as hood as a person could be. He was the protector of the trio. If anyone had a problem with Kevin or Richard, they had a problem with James. He was well known in the streets of Canarsie for all the wrong reasons. At 6'3 and well over 275 pounds, James found that teams wanted him for every sport there was. But James never thought twice about playing sports; he was all about money and women. His name was whispered about in the seediest of places. James had a reputation which had to be respected in the streets. He was well known for his quick trigger for violence when it came to his friends or anyone he cared about.

"My nigga! What's the deal, Kev? Are you coming by tonight? I got this new white chick you have to get some of. Her sex game is the best, and I promise you won't want to go back to the little Asian thing you like so much."

"Really?" Kevin stared at the phone as memories of past conquests in James' club came to mind. "I'm on my way, buddy."

As he passed JFK Airport, Kevin's thoughts circled back to his earlier sexual escapades with Karen.

"Wait, James, I can't do it. It's a school night, Brother. I have papers to grade."

"That's never stopped you in the past, my nigga."

Kevin smirked. "Yeah, yeah, yeah, but I already did my thing for the day. I don't need anything for tonight."

"Oh, I forgot! It's Thursday! I take it you saw Ms. Karen?"

"Damn! Am I that predictable, Brother?"

James' voice thundered through the phone. "Yes, you are. But listen, Kev, I grew up with you, so I know you're nasty. I know you weren't going to pass up on that booty, especially with that lame husband she has. You keep doing your thing, man, I'm not mad at you, Bro, because if you stop sexing her, you know I'm going to jump on."

"Boy, please you think she'll want you after being with me?"

"What? You think your game is still like that?"

Kevin chuckled, enjoying the playful moment. "James, listen. My game has been like that and will be like that.

You know you have a poster at home of me in your bedroom because you really want to be me so stop it."

"Kevin, you're so full of it. You're so full of crap it's ridiculous."

"Well, I might be full of crap, but my game is still tight."

"Yeah OK, whatever, Brother. I'll accept second place behind a pimp like you. Anyway, Kev, you know I don't have time to chase the hoes the way you do. I have entirely too many down here."

"I heard that, Brother, I heard that. Listen, what's the deal with the spot?"

James owned the only gentleman's club in the Hempstead area of Long Island. His business savvy in his chosen area of expertise led to great success. He never put his love of women over his love of money, and he was smart enough to move his club to the best possible location for maximum success. Away from Brooklyn, his clientele was heavily Caucasian. Given that demographic, he stood to become rich by supplying what they wanted from a strip club: women who didn't look like their wives and girlfriends. Many of the men who came were married and well off; as long as he ran an upscale place, the regulars would make sure the doors remained open. With the behind-the-scenes prostitution added in, he was set for life.

"Yo, the club's banging, Brother. I just got four new chicks to come out here from New York City. Trust me, it's not easy to get chicks to come this far to do their thing, but they heard about the money we're making, so everything is cool."

James fell silent. "Dude, where'd you go? Why you so quiet all of a sudden?"

James broke his unexpected silence. "Things are going real good, but I want to kick something over with ya. I don't want to talk over the phone about it. I'm going to come by tomorrow. I'll meet you by your house around four when you get out school."

Kevin detected the seriousness in his friend's tone. "Cool, come by about around five instead of four. I'll be there."

Kevin glanced at the digital clock and reluctantly turned for home.

Ten o'clock, he thought. I can partake of some female beauty another day.

His phone rang. Kevin glanced down and smiled at the name on the display: "Crystal Holmes"

Kevin slipped his earpiece in with a practiced motion. "Hey you! What can a brother do for you tonight?"

A sultry voice emanated from the phone "Hey sir, what ya doing? I'm bored. Tarik is with his father and a girl needs some attention"

Kevin adopted his best Barry White voice. "Do you want to stop by for a little while?

Crystal purred into the phone. "I was hoping you would invite me by. I finished Tarik's homework with him and his father is going to bring him to school tomorrow. So, your homework is done for tomorrow and now Mommy needs some extra credit work."

"Well why don't you stop by? I have to go to work in the morning, but I'm sure I've got some- - -extra credit for Mommy. I'll meet you at my house in fifteen minutes."

"Oh Daddy, I'll be there. How did my son luck up to get such a handsome and gifted teacher? What would Tarik and I do without you?"

"I'm not going anywhere so you'll never have to find out."

He disconnected the call and headed home priming himself for Round 2 for the day. He ignored the small voice inside demanding to know when he would focus more on his incredible skill teaching his students and less on seducing their mothers.

K. L. Belvin

Chapter Four

Kevin rolled over in his well-kept king size sleigh bed and nudged Crystal to wake her up. One look at her naked body and he knew he had to get her up and out of his home.

"Morning Daddy. You put in work last night."

Crystal slid out of bed and smiled back at Kevin. "I won't be too long Boo Boo." With practiced ease, she collected her clothes, grabbed her bag and slid into the bathroom.

Kevin smiled as he spoke through the closed door. "Make sure you don't, Baby Doll. I have to get to work."

Kevin slipped on some shorts and headed for the kitchen Aside from the obvious reason, he didn't sleep much. He was unable to shake the recurring feelings that haunted him more frequently after a session with a female friend.

He poured Crystal and himself some orange juice, he picked up the phone...

"Hello Ms. Jose? I'm calling to let you know I won't be in today"

"Really Kevin? Now I have to pay for coverage in your absence." Her voice shifted from professional to flirtatious. You do realize that now you owe me a lunch date?"

Kevin lowered his voice into booty call range. "Ms. Jose, I look forward to lunch and I'll make sure I do all the things you like. I'm going to miss you today."

"Yeah, right! You probably have someone at your house right now. Just make sure you have enough left over for me when you come back to work." Enjoy your day Lover, I'll see you tomorrow"

The moment Kevin hung up the phone, Crystal emerged from the bathroom. She showed absolutely no signs of their sexual tryst.

"How do I look? I can't have your neighbors thinking bad about me." The excitement was missing from Kevin's voice "You look great love."

He walked Crystal to his door and kissed her...

"Kevin, you always show a girl a great time. You are the best teacher my son has ever had. And I mean the best he and I have ever had. I'll talk to you soon. Have a great day in school. Later Daddy!"

Kevin kissed Crystal again. "Enjoy yourself today"

Kevin made sure he didn't say anything about taking the day off. The last thing he wanted was for Crystal to want to stay longer. As Kevin returned to the kitchen to pick up his orange juice he noticed his Bible sitting on top of the refrigerator.

As he flipped through the book, he remembered his mother mentioning the story of David. Now Kevin had heard the story of David and Goliath, but he wasn't as familiar with the rest of the story, other than the fact that Bathsheba was an incredible beautiful woman. As he began to read 2 Samuel 11, he thought to call his grandmother.

Kevin smiled. He knew he could get two things for the price of one phone call: a check-in with his grandmother and her wealth of information about the Bible. She was a walking biblical encyclopedia.

Unable to get his grandmother on the phone, Kevin decided to stop by to check in on her. Canarsie was big enough for Kevin to keep his distance from his mother and grandmother but check in on them regularly. At 83, his grandmother was the person everyone turned to for advice.

Kevin had learned to lean on Nana's words. As he pulled up to the house, Kevin found that he couldn't settle his mind. His thoughts were on his students and which class he would have been teaching this morning. He was hoping his lesson plans would be carried out. He knew how students got when a substitute was working.

His attention turned back to the beautiful two family home. It was bathed in a nice rustic yellow with a gray paneled roof. The redone smooth driveway allowed for him to ride up to the house undetected. This was where he grew up, and each time he came over, he was transported back to his younger years. It was pure love when he saw Mom and Nana. With no father, these women were everything to him, and he lived to make sure they were well taken care of. As if they needed his help.

He rang the doorbell and waited patiently, knowing it took a moment for his grandmother to come to the door. He heard her fumbling around with the locks.

"I'm coming, I'm coming. This old lady can't move but so quickly."

Kevin laughed, and broke into a huge smile when she opened the door.

"Hey, Nana!" Nana's eyes met her grandson, and her smile was bigger than his.

"Hey, baby. How are you, son?"

"I'm good, Nana. How are you feeling?"

"Well, come in. Don't stand there letting the flies in my house. No one has time to be looking for no fly swatter."

Nana turned and walked toward the living room to take a seat. Kevin followed, marveling at how spry Nana still was. She refused to let her health slip. She walked up and down the block every day and still did things around the house. Her stated goal was to live past 100, and Kevin had no doubt she would make it.

She settled her tiny frame on her favorite lounging place, her chaise lounge. Kevin chuckled at how she looked nothing like the rest of the family. Kevin stood six foot three and weighed a pound or two over 275, just like his grandfather. Except for Nana, the women in his family mostly stood under five feet five inches tall and weighed north of 250. Nana had their height, but her five foot three inch frame only carried 155 pounds on a good day.

Kevin sat in a chair across from Nana and marveled how little things changed since his childhood. Nana always rested with her feet up on the chaise

Kevin spoke loudly to make sure Nana heard him. "I heard from Mom you weren't feeling well."

"Oh, baby. I'm just old. I was a little under the weather but nothing to worry about."

Nana looked directly into his eyes. "Are you still running these streets like you don't have any sense?"

Kevin hated lying to his grandmother. "Nah, Nana, I'm hanging in there. I'm doing my thing."

"Now, you didn't come over here to lie to an old woman, did you? You know that's not good."

Kevin sighed. Nana was the only woman alive his charm didn't work on. "For real, Nana, I'm really hanging in there. That's all I can tell you."

"Kevin, baby, I miss you around the house. I saw you after church the Sunday before last, and you haven't been by since."

"I've been busy, Grandma. Plus, you weren't there last week, and I was."

Nana slowly turned to place her feet firmly on the floor and to pierce Kevin with her gaze. He saw every line that filled her face; her eyes didn't budge from his.

"Yeah, busy chasing those skirts, boy. You know that's what did your grandfather in."

Nana got up and walked to the mantle, where a black and white wood frame picture rested. She ran her slim wrinkled finger over the face of the man in the picture.

"Yes, Nana, I know."

Nana had told Kevin the story of his grandfather's death often as she got older, but this time Kevin felt those familiar feelings starting inside his stomach. In an attempt to make the butterflies go away, he stood and joined Nana at the mantle. He looked at the black and white photo and prepared to hear about his namesake, his grandfather Kevin.

Nana's eyes turned from the picture and toward her grandson as she reminisced about the only man she had ever loved. She placed her small hand on his bearded face.

"Come into the kitchen with me. I want to talk to you."

Kevin reached out to take his grandmother's arm and wrapped it around his as they walked toward the kitchen, the site of many talks with his grandmother. He pulled out a chair for her to sit down. When she was settled, he sat across from her and prepared to hear what she had to say.

"You were named after your grandfather. He was Rev. Watkins in the church and Big Daddy Watkins with the ladies. God got tired of your grandfather playing church and insulting Him and took his life

Despite the fact he'd heard this story many times, Kevin flinched.

"Yeah, boy, I said it. The Lord took his life. However, I believe he gave it away." Nana's tone was harsh and raspy as if she had cotton in her throat...

"I know the story, Nana." Kevin tried in vain to change the subject but remained as respectful as possible.

"No you're going to listen to me, boy. Something has been weighing on my chest, and I feel the Lord is up to something. I have learned to listen when my God is talking to me. You see, we have been blessed with a Holy Spirit, and it's our direct connection to the Lord. A hotline if you will. Now I know you know, but you're going to listen to me, boy."

Kevin lowered his head and paid his respect. Hearing his grandmother say something had been weighing on her made him wonder if her weight was connected to his troublesome feelings. Now looking at the ceiling, Kevin settled in to listen.

"Kevin, you're the only man in this family who's gotten to the level you've gotten to, but somehow you've forgotten it's the Lord who has allowed you to get there. Your grandfather thought the same thing. He thought his running around with this married woman and that married woman wouldn't anger the Lord.

I used to act as if I didn't know and say things like 'Big Daddy was just being a man. I knew all about it, but I didn't say anything. I would pray to the Lord to deliver Big Daddy from himself. I begged the Father the same as David begged when he himself sinned against God."

Kevin's ears perked up like a dog who had just heard an unusual sound. First his mother used King David as her example and now his grandmother mentioned David. This was part of why he came over. Was this a coincidence or the Lord speaking to Kevin?

This can't be happening, Kevin thought. My mother and grandmother pulling the same story out to use on me? I bet they planned this at some sort of intervention. His eyes locked in on his grandmother.

Nana sat back in her chair, which looked as old as she was, and continued her story. "I have paid for my silence over these years. It's why the Lord hasn't sent me anyone since Big Daddy. I have made my peace with that."

Kevin leaned forward in his chair, resting his elbow on the table, determined to get a word in. "Nana, I don't understand you. If you knew about it, why did you stay with him? Why would not date after Big Daddy? You are gorgeous."

Kevin always joked with his grandmother about her being a model in the past. She was a silver-haired woman whose beauty was clear. She kept her hair brushed back to show her photographer-friendly face. Her wrinkles in her skin served as a badge of honor since they appeared regal. To Kevin, she was perfect.

"Listen here, boy." Her eyes locked in on her grandson. Her tone changed, and her pitch climbed just short of shouting. "People didn't get divorced in those days like they do today. People didn't just put a person on and off like a pair of shoes. When you got married, it was for good or for bad. And the word of God told me to stay. What was I supposed to do?"

Nana walked over to the stove and put the tea kettle on to warm up.

"Boy do you want some coffee with me?

"No Nana, I'm good."

"I did what I was told to do as a wife. I tried to save my husband's life. I stood with him in church, and he stopped loving the Lord with his heart. He would do the same things you do. He spent his time scoping out the ladies and dancing with the devil in the Lord's house. Now the only difference is you haven't committed your life to preaching the Word, but that is coming.

"He stopped loving the Lord, but that wasn't going to make me stop loving the Lord. I prayed for that man every day. So you see, when that lady's husband came and shot him dead, all I could do was bury him. If it wasn't for the insurance he had, we wouldn't have this house, and you wouldn't have gotten the education you were supposed to get. Now you see how the Lord works it, Son?

"From your grandfather's death, we got life. That's how God does it. He'll take one bad thing and turn around and make a whole lot of good things come from it. I never found another man who was going to marry me and take care of me the way Big Daddy did, so I remained a woman of God. You're asking why I have never remarried because you're thinking how a person can go that long without sex. When you mature and learn to look to the Lord for more than the physical, you'll be OK. So you see, I have been just fine."

Kevin frowned at his grandmother. He was not sure how to take what she said. It didn't fit what he felt about God. "Nana, that don't make any sense. How do you say Grandpop getting shot was a good thing, even if we were given insurance money? That man took away your husband and left you all alone."

Nana pushed herself up from her chair, stepped over to Kevin and gave him a hug. "Baby, I am not alone. I've had

God all these years. I had Jesus Christ walking with me every day. Where your grandfather was concerned, every night I prayed and part of my prayers was that he would find his way back to the Lord.

"He didn't want to because he was caught up in the women. So when that man took his life, he gave us money that I would have never been able to get on my own. I had no education. I was a stay-at-home mom taking care of your mother. I was helping her to take care of you. Your no-good dad offered us nothing. Your grandfather tried to live his life his way. He left here at 43 years old, but he probably could have gotten another forty or sixty years like me. Who knows?"

Kevin's emotions circled inside him like a hurricane. He continued to listen attentively. As the whistle from the tea kettle roared into the air. Nana turned the flames of the stove off and poured the scalding hot water into an off white porcelain coffee cup with the faded words "I Love New York" on the side.

"Baby, I'm an old woman, and I'm tired. I'm waiting for my good getting up morning when I can go home and meet my savior. Jesus Christ and I can walk and dance and talk all day. I'll be all right. I'm hoping that your grandfather will be there, but I have a feeling that he's not because I remember having a conversation with him and asking him was Jesus Christ still his Lord and Savior. He said he didn't have time to talk about that, the same way you do when I ask you. He said he didn't have time, and it was two weeks to the day. I remember. Two weeks to the day when that man shot him right out in front of the house. I can still smell the food I was cooking in the kitchen. I had just put a piece of fresh salt pork in the collards and added a little butter. Everything smelled good the way Big Daddy liked it.

Nana turned to look at the small window in the kitchen as she spoke.

"That was when people ate pork. Now, everybody is fancy using smoked turkey. Calling what they are doing now healthy yet they sicker than ever. Nobody wants to eat pork when everybody grew up on pork. I also fried up some chicken for him. I was just deciding on whether I wanted to make some potatoes or make some rice. The kitchen smelled great, and everything was just right. Then I heard the gunshots."

Kevin saw his grandmother turn toward the front door as if she was reliving the whole event. Her face was stoic and firm. Tears began to fall down her face. Kevin matched them with his own. Seeing his Nana's tears touched him in places he hid from the world.

Nana moved closer to the front door and raised her voice. "Two of 'em. Blam! Blam! I heard people yelling! I heard 'em say, 'Big Daddy got shot!' I knew they couldn't have been talking about my man. Not my Big Daddy!

I ran out to the front of the house and sure enough, with his keys and Bible in his hand, he was laying right there on the steps. I remember I had never seen so much blood in my life.

The man who shot him was standing there saying,

"You don't mess with a man's family! You don't come into a man's home and wreck his family! Keep your hands to yourself! That's the mother of my children!"

Nana turned toward Kevin and wiped her tears.

"Kevin, I know I tell you this story every time I see you. What I am trying to tell you is be careful. These women you're with are going to lead you to your death. If these women got husbands and they lying with you, stop it. Please, boy. I don't want to bury nobody else."

Kevin, wiping the tears from his face, walked up behind his grandmother. "Nana, I'm going to be careful. I promise."

"I know you're going to try, boy. Just understand this. The Lord has kept you alive for a reason. You have your granddaddy's spirit and your father's blood in you. They were both whores, and you standing right in line enjoying your inheritance. I know you don't like hearing about your father, but I'm going to tell you what he was.

Nana move back away from the door and stepped over to her chaise lounge and sat, waving her hands at the chair close to her for Kevin to sit.

"Your father was a pure whore. When I found out that your mom was dating him, I liked to have lost my mind because everybody in the neighborhood knew this man was sleeping with anything walking. When your mother popped up here pregnant, I said, enough is enough and I made him leave.

"I said I don't care where you go. You're not going to be around here to mess up this baby or this family any more than you have already. I didn't want him having anything to do with you because I knew he wasn't going to teach you anything. Only thing he could show you was how to be the only thing he knew how to be: a whore."

Kevin didn't show it when his grandmother spoke, but he hated the fact he never knew his father. He spent his whole life wonder what his father was like. Kevin stood up, acting as if he was adjusting his clothing when it fact he was taking the moment to stop the tears which were about to fall. His mother and grandmother raised him tough;

crying over a man they didn't care for wouldn't have worked.

"You OK boy? You leaving? I am not finished talking."

"No Nana, I was just fixing my clothes"

He sat back down, and to his surprise, Nana gave him more information about the father he never knew.

"The man had no formal education. All he had was street knowledge, but he was gifted in those streets. He jumped at the offer to get out of taking care of you. He left and we haven't heard from him since."

Kevin's tears dried up quickly. Hearing about his father's unceremonious departure brought him to a boil. Every time Kevin thought about all the young men out there with no fathers going through what he did, he got angrier. A father leaving his child was unacceptable to Kevin.

Kevin's voice dropped to a whisper.

"Nana, can we please skip this? I hate that man. I hate hearing about anything he was a part of. I am happy he died."

Frowning, Nana shot back, "Don't let me hear you say you hate a man you didn't know. The Lord doesn't allow us to hate. You father was paid back in spades for the way he lived his life. Isn't dying of HIV or AIDS or however they say it, enough? When they called here to inform us about it, you were only fifteen, and I waited to tell you because I didn't want you messing up in school."

Nana looked up at the ceiling as she spoke, as if she was looking past the walls to something else.

"I'm sorry, boy, I know you don't come by as much because you get tired of hearing these stories, but I don't get tired of telling it because you all we got."

Nana stood up again, walked over to her credenza and picked up one of the trophies, which stood amongst the many awards with Kevin's name on it.

"You got all these awards. You did well in college. Since you began teaching you have been outstanding with the work you've done and all those children love you. We are so proud of you. I know at that school the parents love you, too. One day they gonna change it from The Canarsie Middle School to The Kevin Watkins Middle School. You watch and see."

Kevin lowered his head as his thoughts raced back to last night romp with Crystal. What would his grandmother think if she knew he was taking advantage of his position?

Nana gave her grandson a kiss and returned to her chaise lounge. When she put her feet up once again, Kevin smiled, knowing the lecture was coming to an end.

"Kevin, if you don't change your ways and come home to the Lord, he is going to steal from you the very thing he stole from your grandfather and father. Now, if you turn to him and ask for forgiveness, he will smile on you and welcome you home."

Kevin thought of the conversations he had with Richard and his mother on this very topic. What was he to do when his life was centered around sex?

"You see, boy, that's the beauty of the Lord. It doesn't make a difference who you were. The minute that you catch yourself and decide God is the way, He'll embrace you as if it's a brand new day. Don't you forget that. You hear me, boy?"

"Yes, Nana, I hear you."

He was glad to see she was about to wrap this up. To him, he knew the conversation was heading to a familiar place.

"Why don't you sit down with your brother Richard and let him show you how the Bible really works?"

Kevin rolled his eyes and shook his head from side to side. "Here we go."

He knew his grandmother would work in something about Richard. She loved the idea of him now being a born again Christian.

At that moment Kevin looked down at his phone which vibrated in his hand. He noticed he had a text message; when he clicked on it a picture opened up.

As Kevin tried to pay attention to Nana and look at the phone at the same time, the picture caught him off guard. A close-up of a woman's vagina engaged with her fingers now lay in the palm of his hands with the following message:

"I know you're in school, but I have something for you afterwards. Can you see how wet she is?"

Kevin smiled and typed a reply. "I am sure we can find something to get into. I might be tied up later, but I'll set something up real soon. Thank you for the lovely picture"

"Kevin!"

He jumped slightly and almost dropped the phone

"You're really going to play with that damn phone as I am trying to save your life? I am sure it was one of the nasty women you entertain. You need to get a wife like your buddy Richard. You have such a great friend and you don't bother to look into changing your life."

Kevin lowered his head.

"Nana, do we really have to have this conversation?"

"Yes Boy, I'm trying to help you. The Lord is touching all the people around you. I know you're torn on the inside. I can feel it. You got Satan on one side of you and Jesus on the other with you caught right up in the middle."

Kevin knew this conversation was about Richard and James. His grandmother had never felt comfortable about James's influence on Kevin.

"Why do you have to call James, Satan?"

"James is as close to Satan as I've ever seen. Everybody on Long Island knows he owns that nasty club that's making all that money and causes problems for the men who go there. From what I understand, it's open all week long. Even some church folks stopped going to church because they caught up in that nasty place.

"James is bringing those women from all over up in there, doing all the things that they do. It's like modern day Sodom and Gomorrah over there. I hear the police are up in there having a good time. That's why they don't lock him up. One thing I know for sure is you can't hide it from God. He is going to pay for what he is doing over there. All of you are going to pay for acting like it's OK."

"Nana, you always have your ears to the streets. You seem to hear everything."

"Well, I ain't dead, and I ain't deaf. I still got some connections out there, and I even heard about you too. Nana cocked her head to one side and raised an eyebrow.

Immediately, Kevin felt like a teenager again who was caught sneaking into the house after curfew. That happened to him often once he discovered women as a form of sport.

"That's right, boy, I heard about you, too. I hear you can't keep your hands off the parents, and you're doing things with other teachers, too."

Kevin looked down at his feet. "Lord, where does this woman get her information from?"

"Well, I know you're sitting there thinking who told me all this. Many of these people you mess with like to talk, and more of your business is out in the street than you realize. Boy, at some point, it's going to come back and catch up with you!"

Nana got up and moved to the couch to sit beside Kevin.

"Kevin, I ain't going to keep you cause I'm tired. I thank you for allowing an old lady to have her say, but I need to lie down. I just want you to understand what I said."

Kevin, filled with emotions, could only nod. His ability to speak was being held hostage by the feelings his grandmother had stirred up inside him.

"You know I love you, and I'm gonna keep praying for you. I really believe in prayer. I believe the more I pray, the more the Lord is going to hear me."

Kevin found a few words to respond. "I know, Nana, I believe in prayer, too."

Nana's eyelids perked up. "Baby, I ask the Lord every night to protect you and your friends. However, the Lord can't protect you if you keep running away from him. You have to come to him."

Nana stood again and moved back to the ottoman. Kevin knelt near his elderly grandmother and helped her place her feet up and placed her hand-quilted shawl over her chest. He could tell she was getting ready to get some sleep.

"Yes, Nana, I understand. I'll keep praying."

"Yeah, you do that. You better pray because when God decides to come and give it to you, you're not going to like it, but you going to feel it."

"I gotcha, old lady."

Kevin leaned over Nana and placed a kiss on her forehead.

"Well, go on then, boy. I know you're tired of hearing this old lady rattling off."

Nana's eyes closed as she pulled the quilt under her chin while making herself comfortable.

"I'll talk to you later, Nana."

Kevin walked toward the door as his grandmother drifted to sleep. This time he felt a little different about her speech. He had heard the story about his grandfather many times before, but never with so much information about his father.

"Why did Nana tell me today? How did any of this tie into what I've been feeling?

Kevin reached his car, still feeling uneasy. He looked back at the house. "I love you, Nana. Thank you."

K. L. Belvin

Chapter Five

Kevin headed straight home to digest the information Nana gave him.

His cell phone rang; Kevin put his earpiece in and took the call. James' voice reverberated through the phone. "Hey Kevin. My dude what you doing?"

"I'm heading home."

"Perfect! I'm on my way to your house. I have big news for you and Richard. I called him, he's going to meet me at your house, too."

James' excitement rang through the phone.

"OK then. I'll see you at my crib in a few, partner."

Pulling up to his house, Kevin was greeted by Richard who pulled up at the same time. After both friends parked their cars, they exited together and headed toward Kevin's home. Richard reached over to place his hand on Kevin's shoulder. Kevin turned and smiled at his friend.

"Richard, how are you going to come over here empty handed?"

Richard pushed Kevin to the side. "What are you talking about? James didn't tell me to bring anything."

Kevin laughed while unlocking his door. "Aw, man, come on now. You know I'm a single dude. You know I don't have anything to eat in the house. Maybe some cereal."

After entering, Richard shook his head and sat on the couch, grabbing the remote control. "Just order something, man. You're the fast-food and take-out king. I know you have a menu around here for something."

Richard laughed to himself as he clicked his way through the various channels on the TV.

Kevin sat down across from him. "Man, wait for Mr. Moneybags to get here. I am sure he'll bring something. He's the big-time club owner. By the way, do have any idea what he wants to talk to us about?"

Richard shook his head. "Brother, I have no idea. With James, I can say it's not going to be good. I don't even know what he has me doing here. James knows I don't want to have anything to do with him if it has anything to do with that nasty club of his."

Kevin sighed. "Come on, man. You have to ease up on James. I mean, we both understand that you're a saved man now, and we both respect you're married to Michelle. You have the kids, but we're boys, and we're always going to be boys. Now you can't tell me the Bible has it you can't associate with dudes who are sinning?"

Kevin lived for moments to turn the table on Richard. As much as he loved him, he enjoyed tearing him down from his righteous perch.

"If you can't have friends who are sinners, then you're saying you're better than Jesus. Remember, my brother, Jesus had dinner with some very sinful dudes from what I understand. No different from James and me."

Richard sighed. "You're right."

Kevin dug in. "So come on, you know that you and James are family. You have to be easy on him, man. He is not that bad."

Richard stood and walked over to the kitchen, which was just to the side of the living room. "Listen, I have to be careful of the things James wants to be involved with. I'm an active member of my church now. I hold a position on the church's financial ministry. I just can't be a part of negative situations. People already question my friendship with you two because of the way you both choose to live your lives."

Kevin heard the sadness in Richard's voice and chose to attack instead of commiserate. "Richard, we both know the church is one of the most scandalous places under the sun. I have been with about four or five of those chicks you have running around in the church that have so-called positions."

Richard clenched his teeth.

"I wish you hadn't decided to go there, but trust me I know. Beyond that, a few of the members of the church have an idea about you and others who are lying to God while holding positions in the church."

Richard's anger increased with each word. "We had to release a couple of people from their positions because of the things they were doing. We knew and they knew their actions were ungodly and not becoming of a ranking member of the church. We tried to keep the problems quiet, but people forget the Lord sees everything. When there were improprieties going on, changes had to be made. Remember that deacon you talked about last month?"

"Who, Deacon Johnson?"

"Yes. He's no longer with us. Actually, he and his wife are no longer together either. They left the church and the city yesterday. Supposedly he's going on to another church in New Jersey."

Kevin nodded his head in confirmation.

"Kevin, it was sad. Not only did he have sticky fingers, but he got one of the church women pregnant. All that time in our church and he was doing the devil's work."

Kevin smiled the kind of grin a cartoon cat would have after catching a canary.

"You're kidding! Brother Johnson was getting down like that? Let me find out it was going down like that at the church. Maybe I need to come to church more often."

Kevin laughed and walked past Richard to get to his refrigerator.

"Kevin, you just come on Sundays and don't have to worry about what's going on in the church. It's all part of the cleaning up process. Pastor has really been on his grind with the changes. This is why I have to be careful with you and James."

Kevin started to keep clowning the church just to get under Richard's skin, but this conversation increased the feelings of fear and trouble Kevin had felt lately. Those feelings were building up, and Kevin wasn't sure where they came from.

"Kevin are you listening to me? It seems you have been drifting more and more these past few times we've talked man. You OK?"

Kevin walking passed Richard to take a seat near him and responds. "I'm good man. Just thinking, but nothing deep. Finish what you were saying brother."

"Kev, we grew up listening to Pastor Ray. After working with him closely as kids. I'm realizing he is really a down to earth brother. He's an older dude, but he's really connected to the streets and to the young folks in his church. He has a strong connection to the young men in the neighborhood, and he uses them to fill valuable roles in his church family. He has a touch with them. I swear it's like you do when you're in school."

Richard walked over to Kevin and placed his hand on his shoulder. "In our youth ministry, Pastor is actually the teacher and has increased the number of young folks who attend regularly. We went from only 15 kids in our Youth Ministry to 45, and in the Young Men's Outreach Program, he has almost 75 kids coming in for Friday youth nights. Imagine that. 75 young men who aren't on those hard streets doing their thing in church, Kevin. Richard says smiling.

Kevin looked up at Richard with a shocked look on his face "Seventy-five kids? Wait a minute? When you and I were in it, there were only seven. All of us stood around talking about what happened in school like we were at the park. I remember we had to get beatings and be forced to attend the program back then."

When it came to young men and women Kevin was extremely attentive. The only thing he took more serious than dealing with women was the love he had for helping children grow. He loved being a mentor despite his lustful flaws.

Richard's hearty laugh filled the apartment. "I remember they just sat around and read the Bible all day. We had to fight falling asleep. Well, Pastor has changed all of that. After the murder of his grandson, he jumped on the mission to get young men reconnected to the church. He has Christian hip-hop music playing and clean videos for the kids to watch. He also purchases interesting books dealing with getting off the streets from local authors and plenty of board games to keep the children engaged. He even sets up talks with the artist and authors who come in and speak to the children so they can hear firsthand."

Richard's smile was bright. Kevin couldn't help but smile too, because when it came to the children, his personal wants were secondary. He looked at Richard with a sense of joy. The reoccurring fear and doubt inside of him reached a different level with each word Richard spoke about the church. Kevin wanted to say something to Richard, but kept his feelings to himself.

"Hold up, hold up!" Richard, you're joking. They're allow hip-hop videos and music in the church? So the church is basically selling out to get the kids to come?"

Richard shook his head,

"Not at all, Brother, it's not like that. Its Gospel hip hop and Gospel videos. He has the kids writing Hip Hop music, he's getting them studio time, and he's actually building a studio in the church. Let me tell you, Pastor is really doing some things, and the kids are digging it. Kevin, you really need to come and be a part of the future of the church. With your teaching talents and knowledge of the Bible, you could be such a leader in the church."

"Wow! I didn't know that."

"Yes, Brother, I've been telling you. Do you ever listen to me?"

"Yeah, sometimes I do, Brother, sometimes I don't. But you know the kids arc my thing."

"Listen, you know all you have to do is go to Pastor and tell him that you want a spot in the church, and you know you're good money."

Richard walked to the window and looked out for James while speaking to Kevin.

Kevin sensed Richard was about to make a further pitch about church and cut him off.

"Listen, I stay out of the Lord's house except for the days I am there with my mother and grandmother. My arrangement with God is a good one. I leave the Lord's house alone, and He turns his back to what I'm doing in this house. We're all good with the arrangement."

66

Richard turned back toward Kevin, eyes blazing with anger. "Kevin, stop! Please stop playing with God. I can't with you. You act as if you're bigger than the Lord. You sound like Jay-Z or Kanye West in their songs. You know the Lord doesn't turn His back on what you're doing. How many times does someone have to tell you?"

Kevin chuckled. "Well, I hope He isn't watching too closely because I've been really into some nasty things these last couple of weeks."

"Ugh! Kevin, please, I don't want to hear it! You really need to stop playing with the Lord. It's a game you won't win. He's not like all the women you bed down who can be manipulated. You're as hard headed now as you was when we were younger. You're going to mess around and get a beating you don't want playing with God."

K. L. Belvin

Chapter Six

Before another word could be uttered by either friend, they heard a knock on the door. Richard moved toward the door since he was standing closer to it than Kevin.

"Who is it?"

Kevin rolled his eyes. "T.D. Jakes, you know who it is, just open the damn door! Come on, nigga, open the door!"

"Hold on, man, hold on."

Richard opened the door, and James entered with a big smile. "My man, Richard! What the hell's up, Church Boy?"

Richard smiled. "Shut up, James."

James grabbed Richard and tried to hug him. "Give me some love, nigga! A brother can't get no love?"

Richard pushed James back. "Whatever, man, will you get your big behind off me?"

"Damn, they don't hug in the church? How's that fine ass Michelle?"

"Hey don't start. You know I don't play that."

"I'm sorry, Brother, I'm not sweating your wife. You know that. Just asking how she and kids are doing."

"They're doing good. Actually we are all doing real good. You need to come by the house and say what's up to the kids. They wouldn't mind seeing their uncle sometime."

"You're right. I should come by more. But I try to keep my distance." James laughed. "Your wife is mean as hell!"

Kevin chimed in. "Yeah, that's true, Richard. Your wife is a little tough on folks." James snickered, and Richard glared at him.

"No, it's not that, fool. She just loves the Lord and her husband with a passion. Michelle is a wonderful woman who for the life of her can't understand how I'm still friends with you guys. There are times she just really hates you two but respects that you're my friends.

"She really doesn't like me being friends with you, James. I had to fight to get approval for you two to be the godfathers of the kids. I said I wasn't going to have it any other way."

Kevin and James looked at each other and shook their heads. James looked back at Richard.

"By the way, how's my girl, Kierra, doing?"

Richard beamed. "She's doing well. Her grades are good and she's doing her thing in school. She's such a cornball, and I love it! There's even a little boy who was looking at her the other day."

"Yo, wait a minute." Kevin leaned forward in his chair, and his eyes widened. "No, No, no. What is she twelve now?"

"Not yet, Kevin. What are you, drunk? She's eleven."

"How is my little man doing?" James asked.

"Anthony is doing well. He's playing basketball now."

"Ok, does he have a jump shot? We have to take him out to the park and teach him how to do his thing."

James smiled as if he was the proud dad. As the godfather to Anthony and Kierra's uncle, he loved them as his own. Richard truly lived a life his buddies secretly respected.

"I haven't been to the park in so long."

James rubbed his belly as if he needed to lose weight. At six foot three and 275 pounds, there wasn't an ounce of fat on him. He made it a habit to remain fit. James felt that if he was going to be in his line of business, he needed to be ready physically.

"Anthony is really growing up, man, I am proud of you."

Richard swelled up with pride at James' compliment.

"All right, James, we're here. What is it that you wanted to talk about?"

Kevin sat up on the couch to hear what was about to go down. He looked at Richard and James and started to get an uneasy feeling in the pit of his stomach.

"I have something I want to kick with you."

Kevin looked him in the eye. "You got us here. Speak up, man."

"OK, check this out. You know the club is doing well."

Kevin laughed. "OK, yeah tell us something we don't know."

"No, Kevin, I'm being serious now. "Check this out. I have an opportunity to get a gambling license and add gambling machines to the club. I would be able to get a financial extension to the club strictly for the gambling set up. The insurance on those machines and for the gambling license is crazy paper. Like the set up at a race track. I have a hook up on how I can actually get the license."

James looked at his friends, hoping they were in agreement with him and his big move.

Richard jumped to his feet and got in James' face. "Hold on a second! Hold on a second! Now you said a couple of years ago you were never going to have gambling in your club because of the element it attracts. Those were your words, correct?"

Richard pointed his finger into James' chest. James pushed it aside.

"Correct. That's why I moved the club to Long Island since I knew at that time a strip club wasn't going to go over well in this part of Brooklyn. Plus I didn't want to place it near either one of you guys at that time,

"So gambling is going to make things better for us?" Richard was visibly growing angry as he waited for the answers to his questions.

"Man, listen. With the changes in New York, gambling laws have changed. I had an opportunity to add on, so I took it. I have financial backers that are going to allow me to create the gambling spot. I didn't want to make a move like that without kicking it around with you because you know what we are and how everybody knows us."

James lowered his head as each word came out of his mouth.

"Come on, fellas. I have an opportunity to expand my business. Poker and other games are hot right now. Gambling is big right now and growing bigger in New York. Casinos are here and I want to be in line for whatever is coming."

"Come on, James, have you lost your soul completely?" Richard's eyes burned with anger; Kevin could almost feel the heat coming off of him. "Do you know what type of ungodly people that is going to bring into your spot?"

James lowered his voice in an attempt to defuse the situation. "Richard, I really don't need the Christian lecture right now, Brother."

Kevin was speechless, shaking his head and staring at his best friends. He hoped they weren't going to come to blows over this.

"Guys, we're talking about major money."

Richard threw up his hands. "Is it always about money with you?

"What the hell else is there than money?" James asked.

"There's God."

"Oh, here you go. God!" James now raised his voice to a level below screaming. "God didn't put money in my pocket! God didn't help me when I was out here struggling! God didn't help me when I was on the streets hustling! God didn't help me through all of the bull crap when I was out there struggling to make it!"

Richard showed no fear. "How can you say that? It was God who protected you that night when you were being robbed. You got shot at and not a bullet came close to you. You don't think that's the Lord?"

James refused to give in. "Hell no! That was me running to get my behind out the way!"

James turned to the one man who had been silent to this point. "Come on, Kevin. Jump in here!"

"Ahhh James, I don't know, Bro. I mean gambling creates problems, man."

Kevin stepped in between the two friends. "Brother, listen, have you considered we have family and friends who might be destroyed by gambling?"

James' mouth fell open as he turned toward Kevin. "Wait a minute. Wait a minute, Kevin. I know you're not sounding like that. You're starting to sound like Richard."

"Come on, Brother. Do you know what type of crowd and people that we're going to bring, James?"

James gripped Kevin's shoulder in an attempt to get him to see the dream as he saw it. "We're going to make millions, baby! Do you know the type of women this would bring into this town? The type of women that you like? The type of women that you can't get? Come on, I know you're tired of sleeping with these ordinary chicks, these teachers and soccer moms."

Kevin held his hand up. "Stop James, I don't really look at it like that. I do my thing."

"Yeah, but now you have a greater opportunity and selection to choose from. Do you know what type of clientele I am talking about? I'm not talking about a shady joint. I'm talking about a real high class upscale joint. I mean we're going to buy the old run down hotel and move the club to there."

Richard's mouth fell open. "What? The Regency? That's been closed for years!"

"Exactly, and we're getting the space cheap. We're going to level the whole spot. We're going to make it so nice you won't even know what's going on inside when you walk around outside. I am going to bring the type of clientele here that's going to put a spot on the map forever."

Richard collected himself and tried to reach his friend one last time. "James, my Brother, listen to me."

"Richard, if you're about to give me some Bible scriptures, I'm not trying to hear it."

"James, check this out. No Bible scriptures, Brother. I'm being real with you. Hear me out on this. We've been boys for over 24 years. You know I have had both of your backs in any and all situations. You know I'd never let anything happen to you or Kevin. You know there was a time that I'd be the first dude there with the burners, ready to do my thing if it meant protecting one of you.

"Well, I'm not that man anymore. I don't see the streets like I did before. I have to be real with you on this, and I'm speaking from my heart and my spirit. You cannot allow money to blind you to the damage you would do to the surrounding communities. If you bring the type of element that follows gambling, you will regret it with your life. We all know that when gambling comes, prostitution comes. We have men here now that can barely control their lives or their marriages. Ask Mr. Kevin over there."

"What? How'd I get in this?"

"I'm being serious. I'm sorry, Kevin, you know I am right. If you bring that type of element in, you know the illegal element follows it." Richard's eyes filled with tears as he made his plea to James. "I see folks in church when we're trying help them understand how to deal with their financial problems and they are unable to cope. Right now with the way things are, we can't create a monster that we know is going to gobble up our own people. That would make us no better than the white man who enslaved us. We then become the very devils I am trying to fight each day."

James' nostrils flared. "Oh, wait a minute, wait a minute. You're now trying to compare me to the white slave owner, Richard?"

"No, Brother, I'm asking you to look at this from all sides. I'm telling you as an ex-hustler. You know the type of drug dealer that I was."

"Richard, you know I respected your game. I still don't understand why the hell you got out of it. You were making good dough. You know what we could do right now with what you were making then with what I have going on now?"

"What are you talking about? I have been away from all that for the last ten years. Don't you see what the Lord has been doing for me? Haven't you seen me doing well?"

"Yeah, I see you doing the church thing, but I also see you're not holding a whole lot of money anymore. To me you're barely making enough for you, much less the wife and kids. You have the nice little house thing going on. That's cute, but, Brother, what you could have had and what you could have done for them is so much more."

"Listen, I have a college fund for both of my kids. I have an insurance policy for my wife so that if anything happens, she's straight. So what I'm saying to you is I have peace of mind. I sleep and know that nobody is breaking into my house trying to rob and kill for what they think I have. All that running around and hustling I was doing, I am lucky to have my life. Why do you think I've worked so hard the last ten years to help clean up the very streets that I was flooding with poison? Now, you want to undo all that I've done by letting that element come back into our lives. I stayed quiet on stripping and now you want to add gambling? Come on, son!"

James rolled his eyes. "Kevin, please jump in here because T.D. Jakes here is killing me."

"James, I really don't know, Bro. Listen, you're a smart businessman, and I know the business is going to be run well, but Richard has a point. If you let that element come into your club, so much could change. I'm working with young men every day. I don't know if a gambling spot less than a few minutes away is going to be the best thing, especially when I'm already working to try to keep them off the streets selling drugs."

Kevin pushed harder, knowing he would hurt James' feelings. "We really worked hard to push the drug dealers out of Canarsie and selling the young on not wanting the easy buck. We shined lights on many corners. Thanks to Richard, we would have never known where to look. If you put this addition to your club, it could cause a big problem."

"Brother, I don't know. I do understand what you're saying about the money, and you have a right to feed yourself."

James refused to stay quiet, crushed by their lack of support. "I can't believe this man. I can't believe my boys aren't going to back my play. I was planning on cutting you in on an extra means of income. You would be able to take care of your family, Richard. Plus, Kevin, whatever you want to do, I got you because you know you'd be part owners."

Richard looked James in the eye. "James, are you not hearing us? I work with the church. I couldn't take money from you even if I wanted you to give it to me."

"Oh, so now because you know the Lord and you're working with the church, you're so big you can't take money from a friend?"

Richard held back tears. "It's not that, my friend. It's how you're going to make your money."

"What's wrong with gambling if it's legal? You're telling me you still can't take money from a legal business? What part of the Bible is that?"

Richard rolled his eyes. "It's not that. Listen to me, James. I have told you before. I do not support gambling because of what it does to people. If people can keep themselves together, gamble, and it not affect them from living their lives and paying their tithes to the Lord, then OK. However we both know most people won't do that."

"Richard, you know, you're so full of crap because the church is one of the biggest scams going. Every church in the area has their offering plate going around two, three, four, five times for this fund and that fund."

Kevin stayed silent as he watched his friends volley back and forth. It was as if he was watching the devil and an angel go at it, and he was in the middle with his head twisting back and forth, trying to find the right words to end this debate.

"You have offerings for this traveling minister, this ministry and that ministry all the while milking the very people you say you're trying to take care of. Where's all that money going? Who keeps that money? You already had two or three dudes you had to let go who were jacking money inside the church. You have hoes running around inside the church that have ended up working with me. So now you're going to sit here and try to tell me that I can't do what I do when the church is one of the most corrupt places going?"

James sat down, knowing he had landed a deep blow to the spirit of Richard's argument. "I don't offer any disrespect to Pastor Ray because I know he's doing his thing, and I know he's been doing this for a minute. That's my man so I can't front on him. I've seen some of the other churches in the neighborhood, and I've seen them doing some of the same hustles that I'm doing in the club, but under the church umbrella. So come on."

Richard's tears stopped and he stood tall to defend his church. "I don't disagree, James. I'm just saying we don't do that at First Baptist. We threw out that type of element, and we're cleaning up our act and of those who come to the church. I was just telling Kevin we have tons of kids there doing some good things."

"Well I thought this would be different so I might as well tell you both. I already bought the space and paid for the license and renovations to the Regency. It's going to be what it's going to be. I'm going to put my club there, and if you cats don't back my play, I'm going to do it anyway."

James headed toward the door. Kevin jumped to his feet and blocked his path.

"Hold on a second! Now hold on a second, James. Now that last statement, you can't just throw that out there like that, Brother. I've been sitting here trying to take it all in. James, please don't just do something for the sake of doing it. I want you to take time out and think about this a little while longer.

If you feel it's what you need to do, then you do what you have to do. We're still going to be your boys, but don't try to back us into a corner. You know we have your back, James. We all are connected to things that are bigger than us. I have school, Richard has the church, and you have your club. I understand your need to make money, but listen, consider doing something else with that space. Just consider it."

"Too late. I already sat down and signed the papers. I already have the financial backing, and I have some guys coming in to work this deal with me."

Kevin shook his head. "Who are the dudes you have backing your money?"

"I really don't want to have that conversation."

Richard noted the sneaky look on James' face. "Wait a minute, James. Who is backing your money?"

"I have the Sunshine Realty Group, and I also have Trans, something."

"Transition Realty? "That new Realty group buying up property all over the city?"

Richard's eye widen and his eyebrows stood straight up.

James' eyes widened. "Yeah that's them, why? You know them, Richard?"

"That's the Realty Company from California! Oh my God! Fool, those guys are organized crime! You need to stay away from them, man! They're ex-drug dealers that try to create legal businesses to run their drugs through."

Richard walked around the living room to try to clear his head.

James shook his head. "Those wimpy looking white dudes?"

"That's mob money, man! One of those dudes who joined the church came from Cali. He remembered me from the drug game years ago and began telling me how they have this whole legal scheme where they create realty companies to wash their drug cash. He was part of their family but gave the life up when he found the Lord. He told me they got the idea from Scarface. They create realty companies and then buy up property or assist business owners with upgrading under their terms."

Richard's shocked look was replaced with sincere concern for James' well-being. "What they do is take the drug money and funnel it into the properties. Sometimes they will use businesses that don't exist or they pay a front man to handle the day to day operation while they clean their money. They find local businesses to back so they can run money through them! Please tell me you didn't sign anything with them, James! My God please tell me you didn't sign your life over to the devil!"

James looked up at Richard. "Great speech, Reverend Run, but it's a done deal, man. I was just coming to ask you how you felt about it. On the real, I don't care anymore. We break ground in two weeks. Within five months, the club is up. I haven't seen anything negative. My lawyer checked out all of the paperwork and did the background research. It's all in good standing."

James puffed up his chest, proud of himself. "I'm 52% owner of everything."

"You fool, if they decide to take you out, your 52% doesn't mean anything. It rolls over to them! You're not gangsta like that, not on their level!"

"Well, Richard there's a lot of things I might not have shared with you over the years. I might be that gangsta. I know you don't come out to Long Island often, but I've made some contacts of my own. I've not mentioned all I do because I didn't want to get you involved personally. I have some backers that if something goes wrong, they'll take care of things for me."

Kevin's jaw dropped. "James! What are you into, man? Why are you dropping this on the table now?"

"Kevin, check this out. I love you and Richard to death. Richard, you're doing the church thing, and Kevin, you're doing the education thing. That's established, but Brother, I thought all I knew was money and women. I've started to realize there are more financial avenues for me to consider. I've lined up some legal ways to do business. I have things in place where money is coming in from supporters, and people are going to run a few things here and there through my business, and I get paid for simply going to the bank."

Richard grabbed James by the shirt. "So you're telling us you're running an illegal business out of your spot over there in Long Island? You have come to my house and sit with my wife and kids when you might have somebody following you who could decide to take you out?"

"Richard, do you think I would bring any of that negativity to your home and family?"

"Are you stupid or something? Do you think you would have had a choice in that matter? If somebody wants to take you out, then it would happen to you and anyone with you. You're full of crap, James! Lord, forgive me for cursing."

James laughed. "Wow, the Church Boy cursed?"

Richard looked over to Kevin who was sitting, shaking his head at the bombshell James had dropped on their friendship. "James, if it's illegal, it means something negative is going to happen, regardless. Brother, illegal business means someone is going to want to wear the crown and be the top person. You might be the money maker today, but somebody will want your spot."

James stiffened with defiance. "Let me deal with that."

"You know what, James, I'm going to pray for you. I'm going to have my wife pray with me."

"Please don't bring your wife into this because then the whole church will know my business."

"James, don't speak negative about my wife." Richard felt his blood beginning to boil over. His love for his wife went without question. "You know what, guys, I have to go. I don't even want to talk about this anymore."

Richard turned and headed to the door.

"Richard?" Kevin grabbed Richard by the arm.

"No, Kevin, get off. I don't even want to talk anymore."

"Let him go, man. Let him go. Let him do his thing. These last ten years, ever since he's been to church he's been a little chick."

Richard stopped just outside the door and turned to James with a look he had never had for his friend. He took deep breaths to calm himself.

"You know what, James? I'm going to let you have that one because I'm God-fearing man. I'm going to tell you this. I love you, James. I will always love you as a brother. I haven't gotten soft. I've gotten wise, and that's why I let a lot go. But, Brother, if you ever call me out like that again, I'm going to forget I'm a Christian, and I'm going to come see you. Is that understood?"

James stuck out his chest like a morning rooster. "Yo, whatever man. Do your thing, Richard."

"No, James, I'm serious, man. What you just laid on us right now could get all of us killed, and I don't want to have nothing to do with it."

Richard turned to his van and began to walk away. He got into his van, but felt called to say one more thing. He opened the driver side door and called out to his friends, who stood outside Kevin's home.

"Brothers, as I leave, I'm going to pray for you both. You do whatever you're going to do. James, you are no longer welcome in my house or around my family until you get rid of whatever illegal connections you need to get rid of."

"Excuse me? I'm not welcome?"

"No, James, you're not welcome in my house. So please, don't come to my house where my wife and children lay their heads as long as you're connected to anything illegal. You want to see me, come see me at the church. Gentlemen, I have to go."

Kevin ran toward the van. "Richard wait! Come on, man. Let's talk."

"No, Kevin. I have to go. God bless both of you."

Kevin heard were the clicking of the van's wheels as the Richard's van made a quick U turn and a hasty departure.

James started toward his black SUV. "Listen, Kev, I'm going to bounce, man. I didn't think that you two would react like this. I figured Richard might have some issues but nothing like this. I thought you would be happy for a brother."

"Wait a second, James. It's not that I'm not happy. It's just that you surprised us with all this. James, you're introducing illegal elements into your business. I thought you were doing really well. Why do you think you need to do this?"

"Kevin, listen. I am doing well, but I have a chance to make more. What's thousands of dollars when you have a chance to make millions?"

"What profits a man that gains the world but loses his soul, James?"

"Oh here you go with the scriptures. Kevin, I'm going to be real with you. You really can't say too much to me, dog, with the stuff that you do down at the club and what you've been doing to the teachers and parents of the kids you teach. Your mouth can't have words on this. How are you going to preach to anybody when you're one of the nastiest niggas going?"

Kevin flinched; James never pulled any punches. "All I'm saying is you need to clean up your own plate before you can question anything I'm doing. I'm definitely not religious like Richard, but the one thing I can tell you is we're cut from the same cloth. You are a nasty dude. You are as hungry for sex as I am for money. You really need to check yourself before you can come tell me anything. OK? Now, come here and give me a hug. I'm out."

Kevin slowly walked over to hug James, knowing he was right about everything he had said. Kevin had fought with himself over his love for the ladies.

"I'll talk to you later, James. Please be careful, man."

"No problem." James jumped into his truck and rolled the window down. "What are you doing this weekend partner?"

"I have some papers to correct."

"Yeah, you get your work done, man. I'll holla at you over the weekend."

As he watched James drive off, Kevin stood in his doorway, dumbfounded. So much news and so many thoughts and feelings rolled within him. He didn't know what to think or believe.

K. L. Belvin

Chapter Seven

Kevin woke up wrestling with the same inward feelings that haunted him recently. He'd thought about James' comments about being the same, but with different tastes and it concerned him.

Kevin had secretly considered himself the go-between with his friends. It was a platform he held dear because it allowed him to maintain the balance between both of his buddies and not worry if he was playing favorites. That technique worked when he used it in his classroom, and until last night had been effective with Richard and James. Now, he felt unnerved over James' stubborn refusal to listen to either of them and also by the strange feelings that kept him from fully enjoying his encounters with women.

He got dressed to go to the park and visit with Richard and family, but decided to go see his mother first.

As soon as he pulled up, he saw his mother in the yard sweeping the walkway.

"Hey, baby. What brings you by?"

"Oh stop playing, Ma. I just called and told you I was on my way."

"I know. But I thought you were going to the park to meet Richard and his family first."

"I'm going by there in a minute."

Kevin's mother stopped sweeping and stared at his face. "What's wrong, baby? You look like you have a lot of stress on your mind. Come on in."

They went inside. Kevin accepted a cup of coffee before getting down to business. "Ma, I wanted to kick it with you a little bit. I wanted to ask you something."

"All right. Go ahead."

"You know Richard and James. We've been boys..."

Before Kevin could finish his mother cut him off, "Yeah, I know. Your whole life. You and Richard were like twins, and James came when you were ten. Yeah, I know the whole story. You have been boys your whole lives."

"Yeah, but Ma, things are different now."

"What do you mean, different? Talk to me, son."

Kevin took a big swallow and decided to speak on what was bothering him.

"James said something to me last night, and I have to admit it's been eating at me."

"Okay. What happened?"

"He said that he and I are the same and the life I'm living is just as sinful as the life he's living and that can't be true, right?"

Kevin's eyes faced the ground out of fear his mother was not going to say anything favorable. Kevin's mother placed her soft but wrinkled hands on his face and lifted his chin up from his chest. As only a mother who loves her child could, she spoke frankly as she had his whole life.

"What do you want, the good news first or the bad news?"

"You know me. Give me the bad news."

"Well, son, James is right. You are living just as sinful as he is. You didn't need me to tell you that. So please tell me what is really bothering you."

"So what the hell is the good news?"

"Well, the good news, son, is you have some understanding of the Lord. James doesn't, so he's further lost than you are."

"All right, okay, help me out here. I mean, I read the Bible, and I go to church with you on Sundays, but I am not sure I understand what you are saying? If sin is sin, there is no difference, so there can't be a good side."

Kevin's mother smiled as she listened to her son. "What I'm saying is, imagine both of you are drowning. You're up to about your nose, so you are still getting a little air in. James is under the water and can't see where he is."

Kevin nodded, more out of feeling the need to do something than from him fully understanding his mother.

"Son, what's happening now is your Holy Spirit is being tossed back and forth because of the relationships you have with your friends. The Bible is clear. It says to flee all sinful situations and here you have a friend who makes his living off sinful situations. Every time you get together, his sinful nature is brought to your table. But you have your own problems. You have become your grandfather, and so without realizing it, James is speaking the truth.

"I know Richard has it difficult; his wife has got to be pressing him about his relationship with you guys."

Kevin took another sip of coffee to avoid having to say anything.

"Kevin, everyone in this town knows what you are and everybody knows what James is, so imagine what Richard is dealing with having to deal with hanging around with the two of you as an active member of his church. I wish I had an answer for you right now, son. All I can tell you is pray because unless you turn your life over to the Lord, you're never going to find true peace. You're never going to find true happiness. Look how happy Richard has been since he gave up that life of crime he used to have. Look at all the things the Lord has blessed him with. He has a house, the car, the wife, and the kids."

"But Mom, it's a small house and the car is an old minivan."

"Yeah, but he's happy. He's having lunch in the park with his wife and kids with that old minivan. He has equity in his house, he's paying on it and he's doing pretty well. Look at you and James still running around here like you're teenagers. James has found a way to take an illegal business and somehow make it legal, and now he wants to try to do more with it."

Kevin's eyes widened. "Wait a minute. What are you talking about?"

"Please. It's all over town."

"What do you mean, it's all over town, Ma?"

She grabbed Kevin's shirt. ."Everybody knows that that crooked company that James is doing business with is going to move gambling in. All I know is somehow the hand of the Lord is going to sweep over James and his club. The Lord is going to clean it all up.

"Kevin, your biggest concern is you need to watch yourself because at some point, the Lord is going to stop playing with you and James, and he's going to let you face your sins. You really need to get yourself right with God. You were baptized years ago. You accepted Jesus Christ as your Lord and Savior. Just reach inside yourself and pull the Holy Spirit forward."

She released Kevin's shirt and fought back tears.

"Aww, Mom, I didn't need that. I just wanted to try to...." Again, Kevin was cut off by his mother. This time the anger was clear in her voice.

"You didn't need what? What did you think I was going to offer you? Did you think I was going to co-sign to your sins? You should already know. I love you dearly, but I love the Lord more. I'm not going to co-sign to what I know is wrong just because you're my son.

"I pray every night the Lord doesn't destroy you because of the way you constantly thumb your nose at Him. It destroyed my father, your father, and it's going to destroy you. Somehow, someway, you're going to feel some pain. It's what's going to bring all this home for you, and you need to make sure you get that straight."

"Yeah, yeah, yeah. I know, Ma. Don't get emotional. I hear everything you're saying. I do. Look, lady, let me get ready to go." Kevin leaned over to kiss his mother on her forehead to comfort her.

Kevin responded coldly to his mother because he really didn't understand why everyone kept saying the Lord was going to do something negative to him. His feelings had not changed. He felt the Lord was not going to make a move against him for what he was doing.

"You be careful, all right? I'm praying for you."

"Thanks, Mama, I need it. Damn. There's my phone. All right, Ma, I have to go."

Kevin saw James' name on his Caller ID. He clicked on his phone to answer it as he walked around to the driver side of his car.

A strong but frightened voice said, "Yo, what's up, dog?"

"What's up, James?"

There was a sense of urgency in his voice. "Listen, I need to talk to you."

Kevin backed out of the driveway. "What's up partner, what's the deal? You sound nervous and what not."

"Yo, can you come by my office?"

"Aw, man, come on. I was supposed to go to the park and meet Richard."

"I understand. But can you please come by my office?"

"Drive to Long Island?"

Damn, he thought, that's a twenty-five minute drive each way without traffic. Saturday traffic means no time with Richard and his family.

"Come on, man. I need to talk to you, and I can't talk over the phone."

Kevin attempted to hold his ground. "Aw, man, come on. I can't do Richard like..."

James cut Kevin off.

"Yo, will you please? It's serious."

Kevin pulled his car over to the side of the road as he spoke. James was the tough guy of the crew. Hearing him emotional had Kevin thinking something might be seriously wrong. "Serious? Are you okay?"

"Not really, yo, Kev, please hurry up."

"All right, I'm on my way. Let me call Richard."

James sighed with relief. "All right, man. Talk to you later."

"Later, man."

Kevin pulled back into traffic. "What did this fool get himself into? Lord, why do I always seem to be in the middle of everything? God, you must be sitting up there laughing at us, huh? Father, listen. Whatever James is dealing with, please just don't let it be anything too serious. Give me the answers, Father, and let me find a way to help him out because he just doesn't get it. I mean, I don't get it either, but at least I talk to you or something like that. All right, Father, thank you. In Jesus' name, Amen."

Kevin smiled. I might not be the church boy Richard is, he thought, but I remember what Nana said about talking to God anytime.

He put his car in drive and quickly put it back into park, remembering he forgot to call Richard. Richard picked up quickly.

"Hello?"

"Hey Rich."

"What's up, my dude? I'm good. Getting gas and some snacks for the park with the family"

"Oh yea that's right. I almost forgot."

Richard noticed the delay in Kevin's answers.

"Kevin, is something wrong? You don't sound yourself?"

"Yo, James just called, man. He's not sounding too good. I have to drive to Long Island, so I'm not going to be able to make it over to the park."

"Aw, come on, man. I just told the kids that their uncle was coming."

"I know, I know. I'm sorry, brother. Let me speak to them."

"Kiki. Anthony. Come speak to your uncle Kevin!"

The sound of scurrying children and panting can be heard in the background of the phone. After what sounds like a tussle for the phone a young soft voice is heard.

"Hey, Uncle Kev. Are you coming to the park with us?"

"No, Babydoll, I have to go do something with Uncle James, so I'll try to be there a little later. But, I'll tell you what. I'll come by tonight and maybe we'll catch a movie. I'll come and hang out with your mom and dad later on tonight."

"Okay, Uncle Kevin! Do you want to speak to Anthony?"

"Sure, put Ant on the phone."

"Here, Big Head, it's Uncle Kev."

"Shut up, Unc. Anthony loved calling his uncle that. He saw it on a T.V. show and thought it was cool to do.

What's going on Unc? Are you coming to play some ball?"

"Nah, little man. I can't come bust you down right now. I have to go help out Uncle James. I'll tell you what. I'm going to come by tonight, hang out, play some video games for a little while. Maybe even we'll order some pizza. When I'm done, I'll hang out with all of you tonight. Okay?"

Anthony switched the phone to his other ear.

"Awww, man, I brought my Jordans to wear while I played you."

"Jordans? When did you get Jordans? You know your dad and mom don't like spending that type of money on sneakers."

"Well, my dad bought them for me because I got 4 A's on my report card and I scored a level 4 on the city test."

Kevin turns from uncle to loving educator. Hearing his nephew had done so well was the ultimate excitement for him.

"Wait a minute. Hold on, hold on, hold on, hold on little dude. You scored a level 4 on the big City-wide test?"

"Yeah, I got four A's too. I told you I was doing pretty good, Unc."

"You know I have something for you, my man. I have to stick a little something in your pocket when I see you tonight. I'll definitely be by... Just tell me what you want. Since dad got the Jordans I'll get you something else."

"Yes! Sounds great Unc, I can't wait to see you later. We'll talk later, Unc, OK?"

Kevin loved his godchildren. Not having any children of his own, they were practically his. He took his role as uncle seriously and loved Richard's children as his own.

"All right Ant, I'll holla at you later. Let me speak to your father."

"Dad! Uncle Kevin wants to speak to you!"

Before handing his father the phone, Anthony can't hold back what his uncle promised to do for him.

"Dad guess what. Uncle Kevin is going to give me some money and buy me what I want. I can't wait."

Shaking his head, Richard walks over to his son and takes the phone.

"Boy you better stop yelling. Yo Kev, what's up?"

"I'm good man, about to get over to James's crib."

"Listen before you hang up and head over to James's house. I have to hit you with this.

I know you love the kids but you can't keep spoiling them and promising them all these gifts. I know you love them but you don't have to keep doing it my dude."

"Man, stop right there Richard. You already know how I feel about Kierra and Anthony. They are like my own children. If I were to ever have children I would want them to be the same as your little ones. You and Michelle have done a tremendous job with them. Plus you know we didn't have much coming up and I want them to have it. Anthony told me about his report card and that needs to be celebrated my dude."

"I know and I understand Kev, but you know Michelle and I don't spend much money these days and I don't the children to think money is coming every time they do something well. You understand I want them to know what role the Lord plays in providing for all of us."

Kevin looked at his watch.

"No problem, Richard. You know I would never over-step my boundaries with the children. I'll ease back. But you already know I'll be there whenever you need me. But listen, I have to jump off and get on my way to see James. He didn't sound too good. Actually he really sounded upset. I don't know what happened, but I'll find out."

"All right man. Kevin, do what you have to do. If you need me, give me a call. I'll be here hanging out with the family. We were about to get ready to eat lunch, But if you need anything, call me and let me know."

Another voice sounded in the distance. "Will you get off that phone? You talk to the man every day. You'll see him later. Will you please hang up and take care of your family?"

Kevin chuckled at the teasing in Richard's wife's voice and couldn't resist clowning Richard a little. "Uh oh, the warden has spoken. Tell her I love her and I'll talk to her and all of you later. I should be good, man. If I need anything, I'll hit you up."

"All right, partner be safe. God Bless."

Kevin was glad that the traffic on the Long Island Expressway was in his favor. It only took him twenty minutes to reach the club. James stood outside pacing back and forth and smoking a cigarette. As soon as Kevin stepped out of the car, James was right on top of him. As Kevin came face to face with James, pleasantries went out the window.

"Yo. What's the deal, man? Why do you have me out here on a Saturday when I'm supposed to be in the park with Rich and his family? You mind explaining this?"

James placed his hands on Kevin's shoulders. "Listen Kev, just come inside and sit down, man."

Kevin followed James inside, unused to seeing his friend uneasy. He was always the calm one who was the protector of the friends. James was always the one who handled his business if the situation required him to get physical. There had never been a situation where he saw James looking unable to handle himself, but now he looked downright scared. Kevin had never seen his street-tough friend like this.

When they reached James' office, Kevin sat on a run-down polyester love seat which sat right off to the side of the office door. God only knows what has happened on this piece of furniture. James walked over and sat behind a large reddish brown mahogany desk in a large reddish leather executive chair. He began to search his cluttered desk.

"All right, all right James, what's the matter?"

James picked up a folder from underneath the papers and removed the papers from it.

"Yo, I should have listened to you Kevin."

"What are you talking about man? What's the matter, James?"

"After we talked, it bothered me to see my boys react the way you and Richard did. Kevin, you know I listen to you and Rich, most of the time. I know I grew up in Canarsie too and care about my hood. I felt what you guys were saying and so I went and did some research on the company I'm doing business with."

James sat back and looked to the ceiling quickly before looking back at Kevin. He lowered his head in shame. . "The realty company I am in business with is a mob front."

Kevin's eyes widened as James spoke. He started to bite his lip and hold back his anger, but changed his mind.

"How the hell could you not know something like this, man? You have been in business for years. You know you're always supposed to check someone out when placing your money with theirs. We talked about stuff like that years ago when we were coming up. You wanted the second club so bad you were willing to sell your soul? What are you going to do now?"

Kevin sat back on the love seat and shook his head.

"Listen man I screwed up. As I was reading these articles, it mentioned a number of their holdings are under investigation. When I saw that, I called my contact and told him I wanted to pull my money out and I didn't want to have anything to do with their businesses."

James explained as he stood up and began pacing back and forth.

Kevin shook his head in disappointment as James' words sank in.

"Kevin, they told me that they're going to create the club anyway, and if I pull my money out they'll make me go missing and do the business without me."

Kevin's eyes widened. "What do you mean, make you go missing?"

"All the paperwork is in my name and if I pull out, it's going to send the wrong message to the local zoning committees. They would wonder what's going, which would cause them to investigate us. They'd have to kill me."

"Don't they investigate this stuff anyway?"

James sighed. "They're supposed to. But they don't, because my name is on all the paperwork. They have come to know all the work I'm running is legitimate, so they're never questioning anything I submit. Actually they pushed it through quicker because they like the business I've done in the past with some of the other business folks I've work with."

"What other businesses, boy? I've never heard you mention anything else but the club."

James laughed. "Kevin, the small grocery store down the block from here, the one you says has the chips you like. There are two laundries in Queens I have investments in and a tire shop in Elmont. This is why they don't ask any questions when I put in my paperwork."

James paced back and forth. It made Kevin nervous to see James so jittery.

"So then what are you going to do?"

James looked up to the ceiling. "I really don't know. I don't have a choice. I got in bed with them and I have to see it through"

"All right, all right. Calm down. Let's think. There has to be something we can we do?"

James stops pacing and looks at Kevin. "I don't know, man. I mean, maybe I could just bring it all to the law. But anything could happen and we all might go to jail."

"Aww, man. How did you get yourself into this?"

"Please, man, I do not need I told you so right now. We need to think."

Kevin eyes widened; he jumped to his feet as if a light bulb went off over his head.

"Yo! Richard's connection!"

James looked confused. "Man stop yelling. What do you mean, Richard's connection?"

Kevin walked over and placed his hand on his childhood friend's shoulder "Remember when Richard gave all that drug money back to the police? There was a detective who assured him the money would get turned in. I always said to Richard you know that dude kept that money. But Richard said he's a churchgoing dude and everything went well. I think he and Richard know each other through their churches.

James eyes widened. The fear which gripped his face was replaced by a glimmer of hope.

"Maybe you can work something out with him, and he can get you out of the deal. But you gotta remember, that means letting Richard know what's going on. If you get Richard in it, then that means Michelle is going to want to know what's going on, and once she hears your name is connected to it, you know what this is going to be like."

Kevin shook his head when mentioning Michelle's name. Richard's wife has always been connected to the church and even though she respects her husband, she never liked James. She never understood why her husband continued to befriend Kevin and James but she accepted it because of how much she loved her Richard.

James turned to Kevin with nostrils flared and mouth open wide. "Yo, man, listen. I understand all of that, but you have to talk to Richard and have him come check me out. He is going to have to hook me up with this dude to get me out from under this mess.

"All right, just calm down man. I got you. I know he is going to hate hearing about this but I'll call Richard for you and make it work. You're my boy and you're in trouble.

How long have we been friends? Plus, how many times have you been there for me and Richard. He owes both of us."

Kevin's voice echoed off the empty office walls. As he took out his phone to contact Richard. James moved to the edge of his large wood desk waiting with anticipation.

Kevin looked up from placing the call and laughed. James looked at him like a dog looks at his master when anticipating a treat.

"Man listen, please don't sit there like that. Go get us something to drink while I make this call. You're going to drive me crazy. Go to the bar and come back while I call this dude."

James stood up and shook his head. "Yea OK. Your ass is always drinking for free, along with a few other things you get for free when you come out here."

Kevin chuckled and then pushed James towards the door leading back to the empty club. "Man just go get us some beer and leave me alone. This isn't about me and the ladies I like. We can have that talk another time. Plus you told me there were a few new sexy things dancing out here. I could use some of that action in my life right now."

James walked out the door shaking his head. "And they think I'm the bad one of the group. Your nasty ass is worse than all of us."

As the office door slowly closed Kevin dialed Richard's number. He looked around at the old flyers on the wall and remembered the sexual escapades he had in here.

Richard's voice snapped him out of his reminiscing. "Hey Kev, what's up brother?"

"Yo, Richard."

"What's up, man?"

"Rich we need to talk. Do you have a couple of minutes?"

"Yeah, yeah, yeah, the kids are over on the basketball court, and Michelle is walking with her girlfriends Tammy and Tamara who stopped by. What's up?"

"Do you still have that detective's information you dealt with some years ago when you turned in the money?"

"Man that was almost ten years ago. But yes, you mean Officer Hilton. He attends a church in Manhattan. He's the Captain of police in one of the precincts in New York City. He's not a detective any longer." Richard laughed. "He's moved up the food chain."

Kevin smiled.

"That's even better. Listen, James got himself into some trouble. It's those people you mentioned when we spoke. Like you said, his deal was backed by the mob. But now he wants to try to get out from under this mess. He wants to end this, but they're saying he can't and if he tries to gets out it will be negative for him. You know what I mean by negative"

Kevin's voice lowered to a whisper. James came back in with two bottles of Corona in his hands. Kevin signaled James to be quiet. James nodded in agreement, handed Kevin an open bottle and sat down behind his desk.

"So what are you asking, Kevin?"

"I'm asking you if it's possible, pull some strings and get James out of this mess. It's our boy I'm calling about, not some clown off the street. I know it's messy but James needs our help."

"You want me to get in bed with that problem. A problem, mind you, I said was negative and for what?"

"Because you're pulling your friend out of a bad place."

"Is he there with you right now?"

"Yes, he is."

James voice got louder. "Why didn't he make the call? Why is he hiding behind you? You know what? I'm glad he didn't. After thinking about it, I don't really want to speak to him right now with how I'm feeling about this mess."

Kevin ran his hands over his bald head. "All right Rich. I'll call you later and we'll talk then. Just consider it because I'm asking you for a favor."

"I know what you're asking me. I can't talk right now. I'll talk to you later." Richard's voice grew softer. The frustration was clear in his responses to Kevin.

James stared at Kevin and hung on each word. He was on his second beer while sitting and listening to the one side of the conversation he could hear.

"All right, Kevin, we'll talk."

"Call me later Bro."

Kevin hit End on his cell phone and blew out air from puffed cheeks. He turned to James; before he can utter a word James jumped to his feet, still holding his half empty beer bottle.

"So what did he say? What did he say?"

"Relax, he said he'll see what he can do. He's going to hit me up later. He wondered why you didn't make the call yourself, but he is going to make some calls for you, my dude. You know your boys got you."

Hope he didn't hear what Richard really said, Kevin thought. I need my boy to calm down. I've never seen him this shaken.

Kevin looked up to James. "For right now just start gathering up all the paperwork that you need. Make sure you have all the proof you need to give this cop when he calls you."

James shook his head yes.

"You know this could get messy if Richard can't convince this cop to help us. I am not going to be punked by anyone and I have to handle my business. If the cop won't help, then I'll call in the goons and we go to war with these cats."

James opened up a panel beside his desk and pulled out a brand new shotgun.

Kevin's eyes widened as he jumped to his feet. "What the hell is that, James? Where the hell did you get a fatigue colored shot gun?"

James tapped his hands on the side of the gun and smiled with his familiar confidence.

James smiled. "This right here is a brand new Mossberg 535 Turkey Thug pump shotgun. I even have a scope on it- this thing could knock down an elephant if I needed to. Plus you have to love it- comes with the name Thug, which is perfect for what I might have to do with this. I bought six of them. "

Kevin walked over to James. His voice boomed through the empty office.

"Have you lost your damn mind? Six of these weapons are around here? Man are you trying to go to jail?"

James turned to Kevin with the shotgun held at his side.

"Listen man, you don't run a strip club, with all the damn money I have passing hands in here and not have protection. You're too damn smart to sound so stupid. You and many other brothers are using these back rooms for sex. How do you think I make sure nothing jumps off if any of these freaky dudes lose their minds after getting off with the girls? All my guys here are licensed to carry in New York, plus shotguns are not illegal as long as you don't make any alterations to the weapon. No way I'm doing that- this baby is too pretty to try to alter."

James placed the gun back into the panel and locked it.

"Now I will tell you this. If Richard can't come through and things get tight, I am going to do what I have to do. These are the only guns I have, partner."

Kevin shook his hand, waving the beer back and forth.

"Don't say any more. I am not trying to hear it. If I were to get caught up in anything crazy I could lose my teaching license. It's bad enough I take the chance of coming here to get my freak on. I don't want to be around illegal weapons.

"Are you listening to me? All the guns I have and are connected to are legal. Stop sounding like a chick- it's not a good look on you.

Kevin laughed and walked toward the door.

"I know you aren't talking smack when you were pacing back and forth when I pulled up. You were looking pretty nervous. Now that is really not a good look on the toughest man in New York."

James laughed "Whatever, punk. I'm worried about losing everything I worked so hard to get. This club and my other businesses are my life. I don't have college degrees like you or a great church and wife like Richard. This is all I have, and I'll die trying to protect it."

Kevin's mouth fell open. This was the first time he'd ever heard James express any degree of envy over their lives.

"Listen man, you know Richard will never let us down. That is not his way. I know he loves the Lord and has his wife on his back, but he loves us. Now he might cut your butt off over this, but I'm sure he'll help you."

I hope he will Kevin thought. I know he'll talk to Michelle about it before he does anything. He loves the Lord and he loves his wife, and what they say, goes.

"James, Let me get up out of here. I'll kick it with Richard and we're going to take care of this. I got you partner. I'm not going to let anything happen to my boy. You know that right?"

"All right, partner. I'm going to be out here for a while. I have out of town talent coming in tonight. There's a convention out here in Long Island, and they're coming through later."

Kevin couldn't resist joking with James. "Just be easy. Get laid or something, man."

"Yo, shut up, man. You're acting stupid right now."

James laughed. They both knew James didn't touch the women who work for him, and that he didn't date often in general.

"Whatever man. I'm just saying. You are the Coochie King- get you some. We'll talk in a little bit. Peace, James"

Kevin walked out, wondering if James couldn't trust women because of his work at the club.

Maybe that causes him trust issues with women, Kevin thought. Anyway, I should drive to the park, but Michelle's girls Tammy and Tamara are there. Nobody wants to fight that three-headed dragon. And it would definitely be a fight. Richard shows everything on his face. Michelle would pick it up in a hot minute, and then she and her girls would be all over us.

Kevin climbed into his car, his thoughts on what to say to Richard. Before his backside hit the leather interior, his phone rang. Kevin glanced at the Caller ID display and dreaded answering, because he knew this wouldn't be an easy conversation.

"Richard, what's going on?"

"Yo Kev. Listen let's meet up to talk. Meet me at the USA Diner on Merrick Blvd., in Queens. It's the diner near the McDonalds, where the bowling alley used to be.

"So you're not going to let me in on what you're thinking concerning James."

"Man that is why I said meet me at the diner! You're not twelve- just wait a few minutes and we'll talk. Plus I'm hungry and they have great cheeseburgers there. So, just hang up and meet me."

"Damn you going to order me around like that?" Kevin chuckled. "I'm on my way, partner. I'm just leaving James' place now. I am about five minutes from the expressway. I'll see you in a few."

"Thank You"

Kevin stared at his phone for long minutes after Richard disconnected.

I hope I'm wrong, he thought, but it feels to me like Richard isn't gonna help out. If he does that, James is screwed.

Fifteen minutes later, Kevin pulled into the diner parking lot and saw Richard's mini-van already in the parking lot. Kevin took a deep breath and headed into the restaurant. Richard sat at the rustic looking table reading a menu. Kevin slapped at the menu and greeted his friend.

"What's up, punk? You got me here. What you want to talk about that we couldn't have discussed on the phone? I was trying to set something up for tonight. I need to be home so I can clean the house if I am going to have a lady over. Ya know?"

Richard laughed and begins to fill Kevin in.

"Kevin do you ever get enough? What is it with you and laying with all these ladies? Listen, I was speaking to Michelle..."

"Oh my God. I know you didn't tell your wife."

Richard smiled

"Man, I don't make any moves or decisions without telling my wife. You already knew this, so stop playing and listen to me, please."

"Aww, man. What did she do?"

"She flipped. She asked me why I bothered to even get involved with you two with this foolishness, but James is my boy, and I can't let anything happen to my boy."

"That's what I'm talking about! My nigga!"

"Will you lower you damn voice?" Richard looked up to the ceiling and shook his head. "Oh Lord, Please forgive me for my mouth. I am sorry I allowed myself to act this way."

Kevin chuckled to himself. Richard had been off the streets for years, but he still found himself apologizing for occasionally cursing.

"Kevin please listen to me. This is serious, man. I'm trying to explain something to you. Just listen to me. I'm going to go meet with the chief. He's no longer a member of our church. He started going to another church when we had a dude start stealing money."

Kevin's eyes widened.

"Hold up you never told me you had someone with light fingers in the church. They're getting down like that in the house of the Lord? I am sure you and Pastor whooped his butt."

Kevin big hearty laugh grabbed the attention of the other patrons again.

Richard seeming frustrated grapples the conversation back from Kevin once again.

"Will you please shut up, Negro? I am not going to discuss church business with a dude who only shows up with his mother or grandmother once or twice over a few months. So please shut your mouth. The person who stole the money was dealt with. The chief left after that situation, but he still has his roots with our church. We have done good business with his church- we've held mutual revivals with his church and we respect the way they serve the Lord. They're saving souls over there, just like us.

"Wait. Did you just call out to the Lord for saying a curse word? You are a grown ass man. Please don't tell me you're getting like the old women at church who have to speak to the Lord with every move they make or word they say."

Kevin laughed, but Richard didn't look amused. He stayed focused on the business at hand.

"Hilton is going to need James to give him all the paperwork as well as testify against them. Hilton said if things line up like James says, everything will be dealt with. I'll call him again tomorrow. I told him I needed to speak to you and get in touch with James first."

Richard looked around the diner as if he had a secret to tell Kevin and then looked back at him.

"Rich, this isn't gonna be good, is it?"

"Kevin listen. I am going to take care of this for James, but after this is situation is over, you guys won't be welcome in my house."

Kevin's eyes widened and his mouth dropped wide open. His eyebrows raised toward the ceiling with shock at what he just heard his best friend say. He tried and failed to contain his emotions.

"Excuse me? Yo, we're your boys. How the hell are you going to say we aren't welcome in your home? Hell I am the godfather to your children. Negro are you joking?"

"Kevin please listen to me. Yes, you're my boys and yes I love you guys, but Kevin, I can't serve two masters. I've been meaning to tell you this for a minute. You know a lot of the things that you're doing has gotten back to Michelle. She really doesn't understand why I was keeping two very sinful friends in my life. She brought it to my attention that I wasn't ministering to you two. She felt if I wasn't ministering to you, and I haven't been, when what am I doing when you guys are into what you're into with the ladies and everything else?"

Kevin looked down at the table and shook his head. He knew there was truth to what Richard said, but he never thought he would hear Richard say it.

"I mean I have been preaching to you guys, but I really haven't been ministering to you. She's worried that the longer I stay around you two, the more I could fall back into the type of life I used to have. Kevin I'm not risking losing my wife or upsetting my family over this. You have to understand that, Kevin."

"Yeah, but Brother, listen. You know we're friends ..."

Richard cut him off. "No, no, you guys throw that friends thing around a lot, but I'm married now and my wife takes a position higher than friends."

"Yo, hold on..."

"No, you listen, Kevin. Michelle is everything to me. My kids are everything to me. I love you and James like brothers, you know that. We've grown up together, but my life is the church now. My life is doing what God wants me to do. I can't serve the Lord and then act as if I don't see what you two are doing and act like it's okay. I can't do it anymore. Seriously, it's actually making me sick."

"What?"

"Yes, Brother, I've been trying to keep it in. I developed an ulcer. I didn't want to tell you, but it's been bothering me now for about eight months. I had been in pain for a while, almost two years before learning about the ulcer"

"Well, you always had a funny stomach since we were kids."

Richard sighed. "True, but now it's gotten worse. Michelle has been wanting to say something to you two. I kept telling her don't pick up the phone."

Richard's voice lowered to a soft tone, but filled with pain.

"She really hates the way you two act, but I keep trying to explain to her that's not the way the Lord wants it to work. She constantly brings up the way you treat women. Kevin she says you remind her of the way her father was when her father cheated on her mother often. He even created a child with another woman. James, she can tolerate because he doesn't come over and doesn't really call too much. You're different. She sees you with the kids all the time and just doesn't understand why you live the way you do."

Richard wiped his eyes before the tears had a chance to fall.

"I know the goodness in you, Kevin. I know what you do in your classroom. I've seen the great things you do for your mother and grandmother. I know that you're a great guy when it comes to the people you care about. You just have a love for women which gets you into trouble. It's like you're addicted to having sex with as many women as possible."

"Yeah, but you know I would never let anything happen to you and Michelle or the kids. I love you guys. I've never let my personal business find its way into your home. Now, what Michelle hears on the street or from Tammy and Tamara, I can't control"

The waitress came over. "Is there anything I can get you handsome fellas? Are you OK over here?"

As soon as Kevin saw the pretty smile on the waitress, he got ready to fall into his regular way. This time he glanced over at Richard as the smiling waitress awaited a response. Kevin quickly realized this was not the time for selfish query.

"We're fine love. Can we get the check? Please excuse us, we have some things to discuss."

The waitress took her cue to leave.

"You see Kevin that is why I made you the godfather of the children. But Kev, let's be real. You always think with your penis. You are always trying to figure out angles to bed women down. What I don't understand is you know the Word of God. You've read it and still read it from time to time. When you read those words, don't they touch you or affect you in any way?"

Both men stand as the waitress comes to bring the bill. Kevin hands her a twenty dollar bill without looking at the check and says,

"Keep the change. Just remember my face the next time I come in so we can talk."

Richard shook his head as he pushed his chair in.

"You just can't help yourself can you? Butcan you please answer my question about reading the Bible. Are you really going to tell me those words don't move you?"

Kevin walked to the door, wondering if he should tell Richard how he's felt lately.

"Sometimes Rich, but I don't have time for that." Kevin leaned up against the van and looked up to the evening sky.

"Sometimes I feel like the Lord is not bothering with me, so I don't worry about dealing with all the spiritual, church stuff right now."

Richard open the automatic door on the van, leaned in and tossed his son's basketball to the other seat.

"See, that's what I'm talking about. How can you say you don't have time for the Lord? He's gotta be pulling at you. The Lord doesn't let you sit there and teach and love children and not reach out to you and offer a better way to live life."

Kevin wondered what made Richard say what he just said.

"Brother, once I take care of this business for James, that's going to be it. All right? I'm sure that, given a few months, Michelle will come around."

Richard pressed the remote to start the engine. Kevin walked around to the driver side with Richard in silence.

I'm not sure how to feel about this, Kevin thought. First I keep feeling strange when I'm getting down with women and now I can't go over Rich's house anymore?

He reached over and opened the door for his friend like a valet opening a taxi. He mock bowed and swung his arm across his stomach.

"Allow me, sir"

Richard chuckled lightly. "Man, you always have a smile on your face. You're going to have to grow up someday, my friend. Please think about what I said about the Lord. You know there's a place for you at the church. Pastor loves you."

Richard settled in behind the wheel and rolled down his window.

"Let me get back to the house. I'll call you later. I'm going to go see Hilton later tonight. Call James and get all the information or have him call and give it to me. OK?"

Richard reaches out the window to offer his hand. Kevin shook it and nodded in agreement.

"All right."

"Thanks Brother. I know you may not understand what I am doing but trust me it's for the best. You know I love you man."

Kevin smirked at his friend "What? Man, go ahead, man. That sounds gay between two men."

"It's not gay to tell your brother you love him,"

"Please, you know I love you, man. Will you just get out of here?"

On the drive home, Richard turned down the radio. Fred Hammond singing "No Weapon Formed Against Me Shall Prosper" faded away as Richard spoke with his Creator.

"Heavenly Father. Please forgive me for my sins. Father in Heaven what am I going to do with my friends and Michelle? You know I love my family, but I've always been there for my boys. This is killing me. How do I walk away from friends? My wife is my life and my health is getting worse dealing with all this. What do I do, Father?"

Tears rolled down Richard's cheeks. While he didn't get a direct answer, Richard felt better for having had the conversation. He turned the radio back up, secure in the knowledge that he could trust the Lord with his problems.

"No weapon formed against me shall prosper..."

Fifteen minutes later Richard pulled up to his home. He took a deep breath and prepared to answer the questions Michelle would surely have.

Richard called out as he entered his home. "Hellooooo, Daddy is in the house!"

Michelle appeared at the top of the stairs. "Hey baby. The kids are next door."

She made her way down the stairs.

"So how did your meeting go with Kevin? Did you tell him you weren't going to get involved in James' mess?"

Richard met Michelle at the bottom of the stairs and pulled her into a warm embrace.

"Baby, please just let me handle this and all will be good. I spoke to Kevin and told him I am going to take care of this situation for James and then that's it.

Michelle smile disappeared; she pushed back from Richard and glared at him.

"So, you're going to look me in the face and tell me you're going to do the very opposite of what we discussed before you left this house, Richard?"

She walked away. Richard followed her into the living room.

His voice grew slightly louder. "I'm not trying to make you upset. Kevin asked me to do a favor for James. I'm going to take care of the favor and then that's it."

Michelle sat down on the large sectional in their living room and crossed her arms.

"So, our conversation about not getting involved with James and about them not being welcome in the house just went in one ear and out the other?"

Richard knelt in front of his wife and put a hand on each of Michelle's thighs.

"No, baby. I told Kevin I would help James and afterwards they are no longer welcome here. They didn't like it, but they had no choice but to accept it."

He took a deep breath. "Michelle, these are my friends since I was a child. I can't turn my back on them now. I prayed about it and asked the Lord to guide me and look over all of us."

Michelle placed her hands on her husband's face and lifted his head Richard's eyes met her own.

"Listen I know you love your friends, but your friends don't respect your beliefs or the beliefs of this family. If you have them around the kids, they'll start to think it's okay to be like Uncle Kevin and Uncle James. Richard, James is a pimp. He might not work on the street, but there is no difference between that and what he does in his club. He sells women. And Kevin is a misogynistic pig. Every woman in the town knows about him. They don't say anything about his behaviors because he's a handsome educated man, and because he does the things he's supposed to do in the classroom. Don't get me wrong, Kevin is a wonderful guy to be around, but everybody knows the things he's doing. I don't understand how he doesn't think people see it."

Michelle stood and walked over to the window.

"There are at least two or three sisters in the church talking about how they have been with him. Eventually those behaviors are going to come home to get him, and being friends with him could create a problem for you as well, Baby. You know how I how I feel about you and our family. When I married you and learned about your past, it was difficult to deal with. I was able to stand with you because I saw the strong work that you were doing in church for the Lord."

Michelle turned toward Richard with tears in her eyes.

"Baby, you're a pillar in this community. I love when I see you doing the things you do in the church. Plus, you are a tremendous husband and father to our children, but if you keep messing with your friends, you're going to bring the devil to our home, and not even you can't stand up to that."

Richard closed the distance between him and his wife. "Baby I got this. I'm just going to take care of this one thing tonight and then I'm done. I'm not going to continue with things the same way with the fellas. They know I'm not going to throw away the Lord's work to keep hanging out with them."

Michelle looked deep into Richard eyes.

"What is it you have to do tonight?"

Richard smiled.

"There is nothing to worry about. I just have to go meet with Captain Hilton. ."

"Captain Hilton. Isn't he the police officer who used to attend our church? What did they get themselves into?"

Michelle stepped back, put her hands on her hips and tapped her foot, waiting for an answer.

Richard put his hands up in a conciliatory gesture.

"Baby, it's not what you're thinking. I just have to call in a favor and then I'm done. I'm coming right back. The situation has nothing to do with me. I'm just the person reaching out to Hilton for James."

Michelle's face stayed stony.

"So you have to go out tonight? You never go out at night unless it's church business. Can't you just call Captain Hilton? I'm sure if James has his hands on this, it can't be good."

Richard shook his head.

"Listen, Baby. I called Captain Hilton's office and he wasn't there. They said he's riding in one of the cars tonight with one of the new officers. I have some things I need to discuss with him directly. If I'm going to help James, I can't wait to catch him on the phone. I'll be back as soon as I am done. I'm going to leave in a little while. I want to pray first."

Richard headed towards the kitchen. Michelle followed, wanting more clarification. He reached in to get the orange juice. Michelle gently took it from him before he could drink directly from the carton (her pet peeve). She poured some in a glass and handed it to him.

"Richard, you're scaring me."

"Michelle please relax. This has nothing to do with me. I'm fine. I just need to take care of some things for my friends. Kevin asked me to do something for James, and I'm going to take care of it. My boys need me, and we've always had each other's back" Richard said.

Michelle slammed the refrigerator door closed.

"Kevin, Kevin, Kevin! You know Kevin is going to be the death of you. You're already have medical issues because of your friends and now you're heading out into the streets to deal with things for them. Kevin is always in the middle of things and it never seems good, unless it's for school."

Richard pulled his wife into a hug.

"Hey, don't say that. You know there's power of life and death in the words a person uses. Don't put death on me. I'm not going anywhere anytime soon. The Lord, you, and our children are my life and as soon as I can deal with this situation, we'll be good. I'll be home as fast as I can. Now please stop worrying and please stop yelling. I don't like to see you upset. We don't need that negative energy in our home. Come upstairs and pray with me. The Lord has been great to us and He'll continue to do great by us because we're faithful to him and each other."

Richard placed a kiss on Michelle's forehead and led her to the bedroom where they pray together daily.

Chapter Eight

After praying, Richard got dressed and ready to make his way to New York City. He found Michelle sitting in the living room watching T.V. She tried to cover her emotional distress, but Richard could tell she was upset by her constant flipping of channels.

"Hey Sexy, you know you're not watching anything. Why don't you go up and lay down and relax? The kids are staying with Tammy tonight so you have the night to yourself. I'll be back and we can enjoy an empty house."

He kissed Michelle's forehead and whispered in her ear.

"I love you. I'll be home soon."

Michelle turned toward Richard and tried to smile. After kissing her hands, Richard headed out.

He settled into his car and headed out, thinking out loud as he drove.

"I hope Kevin respects what I'm doing for him and James. Now let me see, they said the Captain is working James Street tonight. How ironic is that? I am heading to James Street trying to do this for James."

Richard set his GPS and headed out to the Belt Parkway to make his way to Manhattan. Thirty minutes later, Richard circled the area looking for any police officer who could direct him to Captain Hilton.

"They said to look for a brown sedan. I don't see anything that looks like a police car. There's seems to be nobody out here. Let me call the precinct back. I'm not trying to be out here all night."

Richard's cell phone rang. He adjusted the earpiece and took the call.

"Hey, Kevin what's up?"

"Did you speak to Hilton yet?"

"Man listen, I'm out here now trying to find him. He's supposedly out riding with some of the new recruits. But, I haven't seen his car yet"

Kevin chuckled. "So you actually came out in the street?"

"Yeah, man. I needed to speak to him tonight. I couldn't catch him on the phone, and this is too important to wait for tomorrow to take care of. Did you talk to James?"

Richard circled the area, still looking for the brown sedan. He laughed nervously to himself about the irony of a black man riding around looking for the police.

"Yes, sir. I spoke to James right before I called you. He got a phone call from the mob guys asking why things were delayed. They said if he doesn't move faster to open the Brooklyn club, somebody was going to get hurt. Can you believe that?"

Richard shook his head as he heard the worry in Kevin's voice

"I don't think they'd be stupid enough to do something like that with the club not open yet. I'll do what I have to do to fix it first. Listen, I think I see Hilton. I'm going to call you right back."

"Sounds great Richard, I'll be here at the house. I might be expecting some company tonight."

Richard shook his head in disbelief.

"Man you could have saved that information for yourself. With all that's going on you're thinking about some woman to get with. My God, is sex the only thing you think about? Listen I have run I see Captain Hilton. We'll talk later."

Kevin laughed.

"OK Buddy. We'll talk later."

Richard pressed end on his phone and tossed it on the passenger seat as he pulled over to park. He offered a quick prayer as he got out of his van. He walked slowly and deliberately toward the brown sedan, with his hands clearly visible. Captain Hilton recognized him from a distance, and got out to greet him with a firm handshake.

"What's up Hilton? I pray all is well with you my brother. How are things at Mount Calvary? We miss you at First Baptist."

Hilton chuckled. "Man things are great. We don't have the choir you guys have, but if you guys ever want to suit up and play some ball, it will be over for you guys. We have three former NBA players who joined over the last few months."

Captain Hilton turned to the other officers to let them know he'll be right back.

"I'll be on Channel 2 guys if you need me."

All the officers nodded in an agreement and continued their conversations. Captain Hilton led Richard away from the crowd of officers. They walked across the street and stood in front of a closed bakery.

"So my friend, I haven't seen you out on these streets in years. You were in the drug game the last time we met like this. Dispatch let me know you were looking for me. What's on your mind?"

"Do you remember my friend James? He owns the strip club in Long Island."

Captain Hilton kept an eye on the cars driving back and forth.

"Yes I do. He's the big brother I met once at a BBQ we had for the church a few years back. I've never seen him in the church, but I remember him. And if memory serves, you, he and your friend Kevin grew up together. As a club owner, he's never come up in our vice files which are sent out to each precinct. To my understanding he has one of the busiest and best run clubs in the area. What's up with him?"

"James is making a move to open his next club in Canarsie. He has a location near Foster Avenue and plans to open soon."

Hilton raised an eyebrow.

"What's wrong with that buddy? I'm not a big fan of the location with so many churches in the area. But if he keeps regular club hours, I can't see anything wrong with that. What's the real problem, my friend? Pay me the compliment of being direct. We go way back and God knows we've both seen it all."

Richard took a deep breath. "Here is the problem. He didn't know his financial backers were using mob money to back business purchases. In his research, he came across Transition Realty's history and their connection to business deals which have had negative outcomes. Now he wants out, but they told him if he pulls out of the deal, they're going to hurt him."

Captain Hilton eyes widened.

"Hold on, hold on. Did you say Transition Realty?"

"Yes."

Captain Hilton clapped his hands and raised them to the heavens.

"My Lord, My Lord. God is great! We've been trying to get something on them for a few years now, but they're too slippery to get caught."

Richard blinked in confusion.

"Listen Richard, we have a task force in the city which monitors all these types of purchases and dealings. If he is being threatened and we have proof along with the financials, they are done."

Richard exhaled in relief.

"That's why I'm here. What will he need to do?"

Captain Hilton looked like he was about to dance for joy. "I'll tell you what. If James brings in his financials for the new club to show the deals made with Transition, and if he's willing to wear a wire, we can get him out from under this. The key is, we have to get them threatening him on the wire. That makes it a clear case of racketeering. We would then have the legal right to climb all over their other financials, and I'm sure our people can find plenty in there we can use. When you shake this type of tree, other witnesses fall out. Finding the first person to step up is the hardest part of all this."

Hilton reached into his pocket for a cigarette and lit up in satisfaction.

"Normally folks are too scared to say anything in cases like this. But your boy James is far from soft. Didn't you tell me he was the muscle of your trio?"

They laughed.

"You're right on, sir. James is the hitman of our group. Kevin is the ladies' man, I guess I am the church boy and James is the enforcer. I do believe he won't have any problems stepping up and speaking on this. He's too old to play the "don't snitch game" many of these young dudes play out here. He's a grown man who's all about his money. I don't see this being a problem."

Captain Hilton nodded in agreement.

"I'm just looking for the cherry on top with a case like this. If we can get a proof of conspiracy charge, along with a threat of violence, they're finished."

He reached in his pocket and took out his business card. He wrote on the back and handed it to Richard.

"Please give this to James and have him call Commander Riley. Make sure he tells whoever answers that Captain Hilton told him to call. I'm going to call Riley and him know the call is coming in. Have James make the call tomorrow so he can get the ball rolling."

Richard smiled and placed the card in his jeans pocket.

"Hilton you have always been a standup guy. We miss you at our church, but I love how you take the Lord with you wherever you go. Doing what's right has always been your way. I have much I have to speak to the Lord about. I've been dealing with a few things, but I am sure the Lord is going to make a way."

Captain Hilton nodded.

"My brother anything you need, just ask me. We serve a powerful God and it's never easy, but just keep doing what's right. I am so proud of what you've done with your life. I have seen so many go the way you went and never get back. They're either sitting in jail or laying in the ground. I pray your continued success in your walk with the Lord. Trust me when I tell you, on a job like this, I carry the Lord with me every day. We're going to make this situation right, buddy."

Richard smiled. They shook hands, and Richard turned to walk away. He turned back with a question.

"So Hilton, one last thing."

Hilton stopped in his tracks.

"Fire away buddy."

Richard looked to the ground and then back up to Captain Hilton.

"If you promised to do something for someone you love, but you don't feel comfortable with your decision, how do you go to that person and let them know you've had a change of heart?"

Captain Hilton laughs and says,

"Man listen. You're a man of God. Pray on it and do what feels right to your spirit. If the person loves you back, they'll be upset but it won't last. Plus, remember the Lord already knows what you're dealing with and has equipped you with the tools to deal with anything. Now go and take care of your business."

Richard smiled, nodded in acknowledgement and headed back to his van. He decided to call James and fill him in on the good news.

His phone rang before he could make the call. The name DAQUAN popped up on his screen.

Man, Richard thought, I haven't talked to him in years. Didn't think I would considering how fast I left the drug game. Last I heard he's still in it.

He hit the green answer button on his phone's screen and took a deep breath.

"Yoooo, Four Five!"

Richard chuckled. During his drug dealing days, Richard carried a forty five caliber semi-automatic hand gun with him at all times. He got the nickname rather quickly after the first time he pulled it out.

"What's shaking preacher man. You still serving the Lord and crap like that?"

Richard shook his head.

"Man listen, yes I am still serving the Lord. You can come join me if you want. We always have a seat for you in church, Dae. But I am sure you didn't call me to find out what time church service is on Sundays. Why you reaching out?"

This can't be good, Richard thought. Last time I heard from Daquan was a week after I turned in the drugs and money to the police. He straight up told me he would kill me if he ever saw me again. Wonder if he's ready to make good on that promise?

"I guess the Lord needs gangsters too. Still calling me Dae, huh? You was always a tough-ass dude. There's not a nigga in the street who would call me out my name. By the way, it's Killer Quan now. Don't ask why, just trust the name game is real."

Richard chuckled to himself, too low for Daquan to hear. He didn't want to provoke a dangerous man

"Man will you get to the point and tell me why you reaching out after all these years. I have some things to do, plus I don't know who might be tapping your phone."

Richard chuckled, getting the same response from Daquan.

"OK four five, I see you still right to the point with yours? OK, I'll fill you in on why I tracked you down. You was a hard cat to find. I know your wife is friends with Tamara and I use to date Tamara's sister so I was able to get your number that way. You know I had pure hate for you ten years ago for what you did to the crew and leaving me on the streets. I was going to have you killed. Real Talk."

Richard tensed up and prayed that nothing bad was going to come down on his family because of his past.

"However, when I thought about you giving up the crown and walking away, it made me the boss. The money, the women, and all the drug spots came to me, and the crew loved the new direction I took them in. I'm sorry, I digress."

Daquan laughed loudly into the phone.

"However, the hit on your life never came because you had my back a few times. You held me down when I was locked up for the short bid up at Watertown. You held my mother down and my baby mothers told me they wanted for nothing. My children stayed in the freshest clothes because of you. You never asked for nothing when I came home. We went right back to business when I got out. So I called off the crew and told them if anyone came at you, they would have to deal with me. I counted the money and the drugs as, what do the white business men call it? A servant's package."

Richard took the phone way from his mouth to laugh again. Daquan calling a "severance package" a servant's package cracked him up.

Thank God he called off the hit, Richard thought. Lord, I thank You and I praise You for protecting me. I will never stop working to atone for what I used to do.

"No problem, my dude. You were my Number One and I swore to take care of you like you swore to take care of my people. So it was never an issue. Plus you had the best little ones on the planet who had no idea what their father was into. I wasn't going to allow the next man to come in there and mess up what you had in place with the mother of your children. We were family, my dude. Family looks out for each other. But those days are behind me my man. So what's up? Why'd you work so hard to get me on the phone tonight?"

"Sorry Four Five, I'm sitting here chattin'. Listen this is serious. Your man Kevin is in some trouble. Real Talk."

Richard readjusted himself in his seat and leaned forward.

"What happen? What do you mean Kevin is in trouble?"

"Tae Tae was at the bar on Flatbush and a dude came in to buy a gun. You know how we do- if your bread is right, we got that weaponry. But when they went in the back, the dude was upset and complaining he was going to kill someone. We figured that- why else would a square like this want a gun but to hurt someone or protection? Anyway, Cornball said some teacher dude was banging his wife. OK still no biggie, but then Tae Tae said he heard Jimbo ask "How do you know your wife cheating on you with some teacher dude?"

Tae said the dude was snooping in her phone and found text messages and pictures she had been sending to a dude she teach with and said his name was Kevin. So when Tae heard Kevin, he asked "Which school your wife work at, homie?" Tae said the dude said 211 in Canarsie. He wasn't sure if that was the school your boy Kev worked at. I figure I do you a solid; I'm sure even as a church boy, you still look after your people. I still don't like what you did to us back in the day, but I ain't going to let news like this walk by."

Richard's eyes and mouth were wide open.

"Yo, Dae, thanks. I think it is my boy this dude was looking for. I have to make some calls to get out in front of this before something happens. Listen, thank you for reaching out my dude. Respect my man.

"Man listen, you would have done the same for me back in the day. Just remember no matter what happens, you guys don't know anything about where the gun came from. Real Talk."

"You got it, my dude. Let me make some other calls"

Richard hit the red END button.

Man, what do I do first? I better call Hilton. The call went to voicemail after the third ring.

"Hello you have Captain Clarence Hilton, please leave your name, number, and reason for your call. If you have an emergency please call 911 for assistance."

"Hilton, please call me when you can; it's an emergency. I think Kevin is going to be in big trouble and I need your help. Please in Jesus name call me back when you get this message, buddy."

Richard ended the call and hit Kevin's number next, frantic to reach his friend in time.

Richard got voicemail again, this time with R. Kelly's "World Greatest" playing in the background.

"Hello this is Kevin. Thank You for taking the time to make your call. Please leave your name and message. If you're a parent calling about homework or classwork please stop by the schools website and click on my picture. Take Care."

"Yo, dude hit me right back when you get this message. It's a matter of life and death. Please Kevin it's important."

Richard called James next, getting more and more frustrated at getting voicemails at a time like this.

"Call James."

A robotic female voice responded. "Calling James my friend'

As his phone searched for James's phone number Richard eyes were focused on the road. He quickly passed the speed limit trying to get back into Brooklyn.

James picked up after four rings. Richard couldn't hear James over the thunderous sound of hip hop music in the background.

"Richard what's up? Hello? Hello? Richard I can't hear you."

James raised his voice.

"James we have an emergency. Kevin is in trouble."

James gave up on trying to be heard.

"Rich, call me back in fifteen minutes when I am in my office." Richard pulled over to call James back.

Kev said he'd be home, and he had company coming over. He won't be in any position to take a phone call.

"Awww, man! Lord, dealing with James and Kevin I need Your help more than ever now, Father. Heavenly Father please guide me tonight. Give me the words tonight. Allow me to finally reach Kevin. Give me the means to get Kevin to see the error of his ways, Father. I don't want him to stay away from my family. He's my friend and I love him and our friendship Father. I ask the same for James. Please keep him safe until Hilton can make things right. Father I know I speak to You daily. I know I might ask for things daily. But Father, I am trying to show my friends who You are and what You do in my life Father. I know they're not bad dudes at heart. I have tried to use my life be the example to them. But now I need your help to get them to see the truth. My wife is ready to ban them from house and around our children. You know I don't want that,

Father. Father I trust in the end what you decide for me will help me to get my friends to see who you are and what role you could play in their lives, like you've played in mine. I ask this in Jesus name Father. Amen."

The phone rang as Richard ended his prayer. James' name popped up on the screen.

"What's up Rich? What's going on? Talk to me partner."

"Listen Kevin's in trouble. That chick Karen's husband is looking for him. He found out about her and Kevin, and he bought a gun."

James jumped to his feet.

"Have you spoken to him? This is crazy! We have to make sure he knows what's going on. He said he was coming out here, but I haven't heard from him yet. He was supposed to call me after he spoke to you about that situation. If anything happens to our boy, I swear I am going to take this cat out. I mean it, Richard"

"Listen partner, I am in Brooklyn now and I'm on my way to his crib. I think he has company, but I'm gonna to stop by to make sure he knows what's going on. I left a message with Captain Hilton about this too. By the way dude, I took care of that situation for you. Once I get to Kevin's house and get things straight, I'll fill you in on what you have to do. But right now we need to make sure Kevin is OK."

James smiled, relieved that the answer to his problems was near. He slid open the panel beside his desk and pulled out his new shotgun.

"Richard, I'm not worried about that right now. I'm sure you took care of business. We'll handle that how you say, but later. Right now we need to make sure Kevin is OK. I can't leave right now because Tiny isn't here to do the night drop, or I'd head right out there. Imma make a call or two and have my partners stop by to make sure Kev's all good."

Richard heard the unmistakable sound of a shotgun being loaded. "Hold off, partner. If you have your boys involved, we could have a mess on our hands. Remember, I said I left a message with Captain Hilton about this. If your boys handle it, it's going to turn out negative. Let's just get to Kevin make sure he's safe and then let the police do what they do. They know who the guy it and they'll take care of it. I'll be there. I'm not as soft as you think. I have the Lord with me."

Richard laughed as he said this, but he was serious and was not worried when it came to the Lord protecting him.

James laughed with him.

"OK T.D. Jakes. I knew somehow you were going to work the Lord into this conversation, but I respect you. You're right though. If something was to go down, it would track back to me. So listen, Rich. Get over there and call me when you arrive. If I don't pick up, text me to let me know you guys are good and I'll call you."

James hesitated. "Rich, listen man, I want to say something to you. I want to thank you for looking out for me, my dude. I know Michelle doesn't like me, but you've always been my dude. I love you man. Thanks again for everything."

Richard was startled by James admission. This was something new.

"James listen, you and Kevin are my brothers. We have been through so much. You know I love you. I know you guys tease me about my connection to the Lord, but someone has to be there to pray for you two."

Richard laughed as he spoke.

"My friend, don't stress. I'll hit you in a few as soon as I get there. Talk to you soon."James agreed and hung up the phone. Richard pulled away from the curb and started on to Kevin's house.

"I see you working on James, Father. Thank You. Now I have to get over to do the same for Kevin. Thank you again, my Father."

K. L. Belvin

Chapter Nine

Richard pulled up at Kevin's house.

I see his car, Richard thought, but no lights on in his condo.

Richard smiled at the small lights lining the pathway to Kevin's door. Kevin loved the modern look to his place. He chose it for features like the lighted pathway and others.

Richard tried to call Kevin again with no success. His phone rang. His wife's name flashed across the screen.

"I know Michelle is pissed with me. I wasn't trying to stay out this long. I am sure she's calling to check and see if I'm hanging out. I'll call her back in a minute. Let me get this foolishness done with and I can get home and get some rest. I can't remember the last time I was out this late."

Richard started to call Kevin again.

"Hey! Hey, you!"

Richard jumped at the voice that seemed to come straight out of darkness. A slim built man loomed out of the darkness and leaned into his open passenger side window.

"Excuse me, brother. How can I help you?"

"You can't help me. You like sleeping with other men's wives?"

Damn, Richard thought, this must be Karen's husband. Lord, help me defuse this. If brother has a gun, he might not feel much like talking.

"Hold, on my brother, you have me mistaken. I'm not who you think I am. My name is Richard. Please, let's calm down and have a conversation brother. Tell me what's bothering you."

Without warning, the man pulled out a gun. His eyes were wild with rage.

"You ain't no Richard. You're that guy, Kevin. You like sleeping with people's wives? You like tearing up and destroying people's families?

"Sir, please in God's name let me explain. You have me confused. Let me just..."

Before Richard said another word, Karen's husband pulled the trigger.

BANG! BANG! BANG!

The sound of gunfire echoed loudly inside the van even as the bullets tore through Richard's flesh. He stared at the smoke rising from the muzzle of the gun.

"I bet you won't sleep with nobody else's wife. How about that?"

The man backed away, watching Richard grab his chest in an attempt to stop the bleeding.

Richard pressed down on his wounds and cried out to the Lord. "Oh God! Father in heaven please forgive me for my sins. Father please take care of my wife and my kids. Oh Heavenly Father please forgive me for my sins."

Richard repeated his prayer request as he sat numb, unable to remove himself from the car. Doors flew open and lights from different apartments illuminated the area. Kevin stood in his door with Karen. Like everyone else, they looked for the source of the gunshots outside their homes.

Kevin looked at the van and his eyed widened at the sight of his best friend slumped behind the wheel.

"Oh my God, it's Richard! Oh my God! Richard!

Kevin fought back tears as he turned to Karen.

"Karen call 911! Tell them somebody's been shot!

Kevin ran to the van, screaming all the way.

"Richard! Oh, my God No, Richard! Oh, my God, Richard! Please God no not him not Richard"

Kevin tore open the van door and froze in horror. Blood covered Richard's shirt and the entire the front seat. Richard struggled, clutching his chest with a terrified look to his face.

"Richard don't move. Sit still brother. The police are on their way. Please don't move."

Richard eyes blinked. He tried to focus through his pain and the overwhelming fear death was close.

"Help me. Please help me. The guy... The guy... He said something about his wife. He just started shooting. Oh my God, my wife, my kids. Please Lord forgive me for my sins. Michelle!!!!"

Onlookers joined Kevin in horror and frustration. Kevin wanted to stop the bleeding, but had no idea where to start

"Just hang in there, man. Hang in there! "The ambulance is on its way! Just hang in there! Oh my God. Father, God. Oh my God. Richard, come on, man. Hang in there, man, hang in there!"

Kevin kept talking to his friend. Richard's speech gave way to heavy sobs as the tears flowed from his eyes and down his cheeks. Kevin saw the lights of the ambulance as it pulled up through the crowd of neighbors who have flooded the streets.

"Richard, listen the ambulance is here. Just relax. They're going to help you."

As the Emergency Medical Technicians run to establish position Richard reached out and grabbed Kevin's arm. "Listen to me. Call Michelle. Tell her- - - come to- - hospital. Tell her not- -to bring- - the children."

Kevin nodded as the technicians' attempts to remove Richard's arm from Kevin so they could work on his wounds.

"Kevin, pray. Make sure you call out to the Lord- - - ask Him to forgive you. Don't end up like this. Please stop. Please turn away from what you're doing. Father, please watch over him."

As the word leaves his lips the technicians had no choice but to pull Richard's arm away from Kevin as they worked to save his life. As they moved him to the ground to work on his wounds, a tall medium built policeman walked over to Kevin.

"Hello sir. Did you see what happened here?"

Kevin looks up the officer after staring at the blood in his hands and shakes his head.

"He's my friend, sir. His name is Richard. I didn't see who did it but he mentioned it might have been the husband of a friend of mine."

The officer glanced over at Karen, half-dressed. She stood in the doorway and wept uncontrollably. He looked back at Kevin in shorts and a wife beater t-shirt and put two and two together.

"Sir is your place close by? I need a statement from you, and I'd like to do it privately. ."

Kevin nodded and realized he needed to call Michelle. He watched the ambulance speed off with Richard and turned to the officer.

"Please sir give me one second." He pointed to his house. "I live there. I'll fill you in on everything I saw, but first I need to call Richard's wife so she can meet them at the emergency room."

The office nodded in agreement and moved towards Karen. Kevin looked at his phone and the blood on his hands, and gathered himself to make the toughest call he's ever made.

"Hello."

"Hello, Michelle."

"Kevin you better not be calling to offer me no lies for my husband. Put Richard on the phone right now. I tried to call him and he is not picking up his phone. What the hell are you two up to now? Put Richard on the damn phone!"

"Michelle, please listen. Please. Something happened to Richard. He was shot here, outside my house."

"What?!? Kevin, what are you talking about? I spoke to him earlier. Shot? What hospital did they take him to?"

Kevin held the phone away from his ear to shield his hearing.

"Sir, what hospital did they take my friend to?"

"Methodist. On Sixth Street."

"Michelle, they took Richard to Methodist on Sixth Street in Park Slope."

"Kevin, I have to go. I have to get to Richard. Oh God please. Please Father."

Michelle hung up before Kevin could respond.

I need to clean up and get over to the hospital myself, Kevin thought.

Kevin turned back to his condo and saw the officer interviewing Karen.

"Officer, I know who did this. I saw my husband drive away right after we heard the gunshots."

"Why do you think he came here and why do you think it was him who did this?"

Karen couldn't stop crying. "My husband has anger issues and he's always said he would kill me and the man I was with if he caught me cheating. He must have followed me here to Kevin's house tonight.

The officer turned to Kevin. "I take it you're Kevin?"

"Yes sir, I am. Can we step into the house? I don't want my neighbors in my business. Plus I have to get dressed to go and check on my friend.

The officer used his shoulder radio to alert the other officers of his location and what he was about to do. He issued an order for them to take statements from the other onlookers.

The three of them went inside Kevin's home.

"Please have a seat sir. I'm going to get dressed while you question us."

"OK sir, Kevin is it? How many people knew about your affair with the young lady here?"

Disapproval dripped from the officer's voice.

Karen looked up, barely able to stop crying enough to speak. .

"My girlfriends know about us. A few of our colleagues from where Kevin and I work know too."

Karen named the school where they work, and Kevin eyes widened. He was stunned at how many people knew about the affair between him and Karen.

"People at school know too? Girl, are you crazy?"

The officer stayed quiet as he listened to Kevin's rage. He wrote down the pertinent parts in his notes to help with the case. Kevin stepped into the bathroom to wash his hands, still railing at Karen.

"You know any one of those folks could have said the wrong thing and blown this whole mess up. Why did you tell so many people? You brought this mess on both of us!"

Karen wailed uncontrollably again.

The officer reasserted control over the situation. "Ma'am, I need you to calm down. Is there anything else you can tell me about what happened? How did your husband know to come here?"

Karen looked at the officer, at Kevin and back at the officer.

"My husband Jermain found out about Kevin and me. He went through my phone and found pictures I sent Kevin and pictures Kevin sent me."

Kevin's eyes got even wider, and his nostrils flared. "What?!? You're joking! Why the hell didn't you say something to me? Why did you keep that to yourself?"

Karen stopped her tears by sheer force of will. "I was going to tell you tonight, but one thing led to another. I figured I would tell you when we were done. I didn't know he was going to shoot your friend. I didn't know what to do. He's always threatened me, but never did anything about it."

Kevin's eyes burned with rage.

"You mean to tell me, you came over here and had sex with me knowing your deranged husband was out looking for me? You didn't even give me a chance to protect myself or my friends! We could have stopped this. Get the hell out of my house! Now! Get the hell out!"

The officer stepped in again and shut down the conversation. Karen slipped on her sweatpants and top, grabbed her things quickly and headed for the door.

"Kevin, Baby, I am so sorry."

"Go to hell. If something happens to my friend, it's on you. Get the hell out."

The office led Karen to the door and watched her walk out. He signaled a fellow officer to walk her to her car and get all her personal information. He turned back to Kevin, who was putting his wallet in his pocket and grabbing his car keys.

"Sir, it's not my place, but I am going to say this anyway. You're yelling at her about your friend being shot tonight, yet you were the one who caused it by sleeping with another man's wife. I'm truly sorry to hear about your friend, but the Lord doesn't take kindly to things like that."

Kevin's eyes widened at the disapproval in the officer's voice.

"Thank you Joel Osteen. You're right- it's NOT your place your place to say anything about my affairs. Go find the dude who shot my best friend. Who are you to judge me or tell me anything about what I am doing and to who? Is there anything else you need from me, because I need to get to the hospital? If you'll excuse me."

Kevin shouldered past the officer, waited for him to leave the house and locked the door.

The officer offered a final word. "Kevin, I've been doing this job for ten years now. I know this- when a man messes with another man's wife or children, bad things happen. You might hate what I'm saying, but as a teacher, I'm sure you know right from wrong. I'll contact you later, sir."

Kevin stormed away and got in his car. As he started his car, he looked back at the officer. A familiar feeling returned as he sped off.

Chapter Ten

Kevin parked in the first space he could find and ran up to the emergency room door. He paused before entering, afraid of what he might hear.

"Hello I need information on Richard Curtis. He was brought in with gun shots to his chest about an hour ago."

The triage nurse checked her computer. At the same time Kevin tried unsuccessfully to call Michelle for an update.

"Sir, he's in surgery. His wife is here, and we only allow one person in the emergency room bed area." Kevin shook his head.

"Please Ms., my best friend could be laying in there dying. I need to see him. Can you please allow me to at least see his wife so I can talk to her? I know one person is the rule but I need this, miss. Please allow me to speak to someone."

"Sir, what is your name?"

He told her.

"Sir, I can't let you go back there, nor can I give you any further information. Mrs. Curtis left strict instructions that you and another individual are not to be permitted access. The best I can do for you is let you wait for her in the waiting area. It's her choice whether or not she tells you anything,

Kevin's shoulders slumped as he sat down in the waiting area. The area was full with members of Richard's church who gathered in prayer. Some of them cast disapproving looks at Kevin and went back to their prayer circle.

Feeling defeated, Kevin walked outside and down the block to gather his thoughts. He found a granite slab to rest on and looked up to the sky.

"My God. Oh my God. What am I going to do? Father in Heaven, I know I played around my whole life. Please don't take Richard, Father. Take me. Please don't take him from those kids. Please don't take him from his wife. Father, please. Not Richard. Oh God, not Richard. Not for my sins, Father."

As the tears flowed harder than they had all evening, Kevin could barely see the moonlight through his tears.

I have to get back in there, he thought. Maybe I can find a way to see him. He might die. I have to see him.

His return to the waiting area was met by one of the church women coming outside.

"Sister what's the word on Richard? What's the news?

She fell forward into Kevin's arms, wailing as if broken. Kevin held up the medium build, middle aged women and let her cry until she could speak.

"He didn't make it. He was shot up too bad- they tried to get the bullets out- - -."

She broke down again and composed herself. "They said after the surgery, he woke up. They said he was talking to his wife. He said a couple of things and then his heart stopped beating. They said they've never seen anything like this. The chaplain is talking with Sister Michelle in the chapel."

Kevin fought back tears as he looked the woman in the eye.

"Thank you for sharing, but I need to go in and see him."

He helped the woman to a seat on the nearest bench and turned the corner. He saw a few squad cars parked where the ambulances usually sat. The same officer Kevin spoke to at his house made eye contact with him first. He walked over.

"Kevin, I am going to need you to come with me. We are going to need your official statement. This has become a murder investigation now and we need to move forward quickly. We picked up Karen's husband at his home. We have to get stated with the paperwork. I'm sorry to hear about your friend passing, but now we have to grant him justice."

K. L. Belvin

Chapter Eleven

Ten days after the murder, Kevin prepared for another difficult moment.

I thought the night Richard was killed was tough, he thought, but now I have to stand here at his funeral. It's my fault he's dead, and everybody here knows it.

He straightened his tie with shaking hands and headed to his car.

He looked up at the overcast sky. "I wish I could trade place with you, Richard. This is crazy; you're no long here to preach to me, joke with me, or point me in the right direction. What do I say to Michelle and the children?"

Before Kevin could take another step away from his condo, an expensive black GMC Yukon XL, with chrome siding and chrome wheels measuring in at twenty four inches slowly rolls up to the sidewalk to a stop. James emerged from the truck with an empty look on his face.

"I've been trying to call you man. Why haven't you answered my calls? Don't do this to me man. You know I'm hurting too."

Kevin stepped forward to hug his friend.

"I'm sorry, brother. I haven't been feeling up to doing anything. Michelle wouldn't speak to me and that is expected. I took time off from work to get my head right."

James placed his right hand on Kevin's shoulder to comfort him.

"Listen, Kev. There is no way you can blame yourself for what happened. You didn't know her husband was going to come blasting like that."

James stepped back and leaned back onto his truck and took out an electronic cigarette. As he inhaled and then exhaled the smoke, he looked at Kevin trying to figure out what to say to get his friend back.

"Listen I got some good news from Richard's police friend. It looks like they are going to be able to help a brother out. I'm going to have to turn into a snitch but I'll do what I have to in order to save my club."

Kevin tried and failed to smile at James' good news.

"James I am glad to hear that, man. Richard always made sure we were looked after. He would be happy to hear that."

"You don't seem dressed for the funeral. Aren't you going?"

James blew smoke upward and looks down before speaking.

"Listen Kevin, you know church folks and I don't get along. Plus Michelle definitely doesn't like me. I really don't want to be a part of that scene. I'll make sure I send gifts and take care of Rich's kids,but right now is not the time."

"What! Man, how can you be selfish at a time like this. Things are turned upside down and you are only thinking about you. That is a sucker's move. You need to be ashamed of yourself for even letting that come out of your mouth!"

Kevin's eyes blazed with rage as he hurled insults at James. James was startled, but didn't flinch. He continued smoking.

"I am going to let that pass because I know you're hurting, my dude. But don't ever get it twisted. Don't ever get in my face and call me a sucker. You know damn well I don't let anyone talk trash about me. So you get a pass this time. Listen, take the time you need to get your head right. I am here for you and you know I love you. We're going to get past this. Rich wouldn't want us to be going at it, so I am going to bounce."

James slid aside to allow Kevin to back up and calm down. Kevin remembered who he was dealing with, took a step back and sought to calm things down.

"I'm sorry James. I wasn't trying to disrespect you. I'm hurting, and I don't need you not there for me right now. I'll see Michelle and the children later. When there is an opening to smooth things over, I'll speak to Michelle about you. But that's if she even speaks to me. So my brother, I don't really know what's going to happen today or after."

As the sun slid behind a band of clouds, the lighting grew dull.

"I'm out, James. I want to get there a little early so I can- -view."

No way I'm telling him I won't stay, Kevin thought. I'm just going to pay my last respects and leave. I'll try to talk to Michelle later.

James hopped into his truck, and leaned out to say one final thing.

"Kevin, remember family, don't let this beat you up. Richard went to church. You know he's up there in Heaven and God is going to take great care of him. Now you and me, we better worry, I don't see either one of us making it through those shiny gates when it's our time. This is why you better hump as much as you can. Make as much paper as you can take from the D.O.E. and enjoy yourself. No one is promised tomorrow."

Kevin watched James pull away and felt the familiar feelings return. James' words frightened him, and he felt an overwhelming desire to call Nana.

"Call grandmother."

His phone answered.

"Calling grandmother."

"Hello"

"Hey, old lady. I'm sure you're mad at me. Allow me to apologize for not calling you back the other day."

"It's okay, boy. Your mother has been by and we had a conversation. We both knew you needed time to deal with all this. I can't believe that boy is dead."

Nana sat in her kitchen waiting for her daughter to take her to the funeral.

"Boy I want you to listen. I know you're hurting about your friend. I know you're blaming yourself for what happened, and you should. Because you were wrong."

Kevin started to say something, but Nana cut him off.

"Now pay attention. You knew damn well what you were doing with that man's wife. I told you everyone in town knew. You would have to be crazy to think that man wasn't going to find out. What you did was underestimate that man's level of crazy. Your grandfather did the same thing, bopping down the street stinking of that man's wife and not thinking anything would happen to him. I smelled it as he lay there dying. After those bullets ripped through his body, he knew the only thing he could do was call out to the Lord to apologize for his sins."

"Wait Nana, what do you mean apologize to the Lord? He didn't say he was sorry to you in those last moments? That is just stupid."

Nana slammed her hand down onto the table.

"Boy what the hell are you talking about. This is the problem with you young folks. You don't go to church anymore and you don't know the Word of the Lord. Now shut your mouth and listen here. In those last few minutes, your grandfather knew he was laying there dying because he sinned with that man's wife. He also knew he had taken a pledge to serve the Lord. He knew in a matter of minutes he was going to meet the Creator face to face, and he wanted to be forgiven. You see boy, that's what makes our Father in Heaven special. If you come to him with open arms and honest heart, He'll forgive you. You have two things to do. You have to apologize to the Lord and apologize to Michelle for taking her husband from her and those children."

Kevin drove with one hand and wiped tears with the other as he listened to Nana.

"Nana, I don't know what to do. I can't go to that woman and look her in the face and say I'm sorry. Plus you know the Lord and I don't have that type of relationship. I wouldn't know the first thing to say."

Nana stood looking out at the same area where her husband died years ago.

"You're going to church, which means you'll be in the right place to speak to God. As for Michelle, you're going to have to wait until she gives you a chance- if she ever does. Remember this, there is never a bad time to lean on God. Hold on to this scripture:

2 Corinthians 5:17, "Therefore if any man be in Christ, he is a new creature: old things are passed away; behold, all things are become new."

So if when you get to church take time to get closer to the Lord. Let the pain go and give it to the Father. Now let me get off this phone and get dressed."

"Thanks Nana. I'll figure something out. I'm not sure what I am going to do but I am listening. Thank you as always. Love you. I'll see you later."

Kevin continued to the church, overwhelmed with emotions and knowing something had to happen to get him through the day.

Chapter Twelve

Kevin pulled into the church parking lot, hoping he arrived early enough not to be seen by too many church people.

They blame me for Richard's death, he though. I do too.

I have no idea how I am going to make it. All these people are acting like I did it. What's even crazier is I haven't heard from Pastor Ray either. That is not a good sign. The way I feel I hope I don't see him right now either.

Kevin saw a large sister next to the sign-in book. He couldn't remember her name.

"Well, look who it is. The Prodigal Son has returned. I was sure we would see you, but my bet was you were going to sneak in during the service and leave before it's over like you did on the few Sundays you've showed up."

She adjusted her bright white gloves, laid the pen down by the sign in book and gestured to it as if demanding proof that Kevin was actually there.   Kevin looked at her and stood up straight.   I am not going to be treated like this all day, he thought this stops right here.

"Excuse me, Ms. I am sorry I don't remember your name. I don't remember you coming over to speak to my mother or grandmother when I was here with them. Can you please show me where Richard's body is placed? I would like to say goodbye to my friend. There will be more than enough time to judge me when I return."

Clearly taken aback, the church sister pointed to a door to the left side of the pulpit. "He's in that back room right now. They are going to place him upfront in an hour or so for the people to say their goodbyes."

Her face was filled with disapproval, but she didn't say another word as Kevin walked away.

Kevin walked closer to the door, feeling as though Richard would come through the door and tell him it was all a joke. He bit his lip to keep his heart rate down as he walked through the door.

Richard lay in an onyx laced coffin with chiffon trim. Kevin couldn't hold back his tears. He realized he'd spent his whole life thinking only about himself, and that he never let the words of life that Richard shared with him sink in deeply enough to change his life.

Kevin looked down at the consequences of his actions: his friend lying dead in front of him.

"Father, why? Why would you take Richard after all the evil I've done? Why, after all the things I've been a part of or I should have never even thought about doing, you spared me? Why? Why would you spare me and take Richard? Richard has a family. A lovely wife who loves him with all her heart. Two children."

Kevin looked to the church ceiling. The custom window panes seemed to shift the light directly where Kevin stood. It went unnoticed to him, as he was wrapped up in his tears and his pain.

"I've watched him raise his children to be respectful and well mannered. They know you, Father. God, why? He christened both of those children right here in this church. I stood there with him. I can still see the water Pastor Ray poured on each of their foreheads speaking in your name. Why would you take him? Why would you allow my sins to touch his home? My God, Father. How did we get here?

Richard left the drugs behind him. He served you daily with everything he had. He tried to get me to see you and understand you. None of this makes any sense. What type of God would do something like this to such a good man?"

Kevin wiped his face with his handkerchief. At that moment, Michelle walked in with tears in her eyes. Her caramel-colored face was drab, and worry was set in her face. She looked directly into Kevin's eyes as they stood in front of her husband's lifeless body.

"Hello, Kevin. They told me I'd find you here. I wanted to come and speak to you."

Kevin turned to face her and reached out his hand as if to make a peaceful gesture. Michelle didn't move a muscle. Kevin's hand is left suspended out in front of him; left hanging, Kevin lowered his hand.

"Michelle, listen. I just..."

"Don't speak. Let me finish, Kevin, and then I'll listen to whatever you have to say."

"Yes, love."

She pointed at Richard and then at Kevin. "Richard spent many nights worrying about you. You understand that, right?"

"Yes, I know."

"Richard's worry was not if you were going to be okay. His worry was if you didn't see your way to what God wanted, you were going to hurt someone because of how close people would get to you. How close the women would get to you. How close your students would get to you. Many a night, when Richard and I sat and talked, we prayed together for you. We prayed that the Father in Heaven would deliver you from the lifestyle you were living because we both knew the power and talents you have inside you."

"God has given you awesome gifts, Kevin. You may not realize this, but I think you do when you're standing in front of a classroom. You capture your students' attention. I've watched you at meetings. I've watched how parents are captivated by what you say. I've seen you with our children. They love their uncle. Richard knew if you could ever get past the flesh, you would go on to great things in God's name. James never understood that, but Richard understood from a very early age. He said your gifts were seen even back then in how you dealt with people, especially girls."

Michelle took a padded chair and sat down

"But let me..."

"No Kevin, I asked you to let me finish. At the hospital before Richard passed, I was with him to the very last breath. I knew he was not going to survive the gunshots. The Lord placed it on my heart to be prepared with the idea I was going to be without Richard. I have to be honest with you, I wasn't ready."

Michelle stood up and walked past Kevin. She looked down at Richard and placed her hands on his face. As her tears bathed each of his cheeks, she tried to wipe them away as fast as they fell.

"Kevin, I was in that hospital room watching them trying to stabilize Richard and trying to keep him from slipping away. My body and soul started to fill with hate for you. I said to myself, Father, why would you take mine after all the things Kevin has done? Then it happened."

"It was as if the Lord bypassed me and touched Richard. He opened his eyes and turned to me and took my hand. In his last breath, he said, 'Don't worry, Honey, I'm going to be okay. Tell our children Daddy loves them.

Michelle listen. Kevin will not let anything happen to you and the children. You can count on him for that. He will make sure the children are always protected. I didn't make him the godfather for no reason. I know the Lord will bring Kevin home because there's greatness in him for the Lord. Remember the Lord says to love your enemies and Kevin is far from an enemy he's just lost. The Lord and all the angels celebrate when someone like Kevin finds their way home

Michelle ran her hand towel over her face. She fought a losing battle to keep up with her tears.

"Before I could even disagree with him, he slipped away. So, the reason I came here to speak to you was out of respect for my husband and respect of the Lord. I didn't take your calls this past week because I wanted to look you in the eye and tell you."

She moved closer to Kevin, grabbed his jacket, bit her lip and took a deep breath.

"Kevin, I forgive you. I still love you, I want you around my children, I want you in my children's lives because they're going to need their uncle even more now because their father is now gone. I don't blame you. I don't care anymore that Richard lost his life trying to protect you because that's what friends do. That was the man he was and would have done the same for anyone he cared for. I wanted to make sure you don't take this the wrong way. The Lord has given you another chance and I pray Richard's death is not in vain. Do you understand me?"

"Yes, Chelle." Kevin spoke just above a whisper.

Michelle started to leave, but turned back to speak.

"I didn't expect you to say anything. I wanted you to hear that."

Kevin nodded as Michelle walked away. He couldn't get the words out that he'd intended to say to her.

Chapter Thirteen

Kevin turned back to his friend.

"Well, my brother, again I want to say I'm so sorry. I know you wouldn't have been at my house that night if it weren't for me. Brother, I'm going to make this vow to you, to Michelle, to Anthony, to Kierra, and to the Lord, I will never let something happen to them even if it takes my life."

Kevin took the chair Michelle vacated and moved it to the head of the coffin.

"Your son will remember who you are. I will make sure of this; every day I will be the example you set for your son. I will be the father figure your daughter needs. No dude will get close without me checking them our thoroughly. She will grow loved by a man who will care for her. I will keep an eye on Michelle to make sure she is protected. I am there, brother. You know James will be there too. Michelle won't like it, but you know James is still the muscle of the crew. He was too scared of your wife to come by with me."

Kevin stood and turned to the large crucifix hanging on the wall with a replica of Jesus on the cross just to his right.

He closed his eyes. "God, I know you're listening. I know You allow things to happen for reasons only You understand. I remember hearing my grandmother say that years ago. I don't remember where the scripture is, I just remember hearing her saying it. "Lean not on your own understanding but trust in the Lord" is what she would say.

"Father, I've known You but I don't know if I trusted you because I couldn't see past myself. Well Father I'm trying to trust You now. I don't know what else to do. I don't have any answers. So Father, I ask that you forgive me for my sins."

Kevin took a deep breath. "Father I ask you to wash away what I've done until this moment. You've kept me here to see this and now I see it. Father, I'm not going to question why you have allowed me to see what I saw. I just ask you grant me the strength and the wisdom to be the man so many people have seen in me. Father, I'm sorry for all that I've have done, and I ask you to place it on my heart and show me what it is I need to do to make things right."

Kevin continued as tears fell.

"I will disconnect from every parent I've had anything with sexually. I'll start coming to your house, Father. I know my mother would like that. She's been dying to get me to come to church on a regular basis, so I'll come. I'll come with her. I'll also bring the kids and Michelle. Father, if I could ask one more thing, could you please tell Richard I'm going to miss him? I wish he was here with me to see this because he always said the day was going to come. He would say there will come a time when You were going to touch me in some way to open my eyes to the way I had been living. Father, I didn't know the payment for my sins was going to be Richard's life. God... God... In Jesus' name, Amen."

As the sun light fell behind a cloud and lighting in the room changed, Kevin saw movement behind him...

"Pastor Ray!" Kevin wondered how much the pastor heard.

Pastor Ray stood about five feet nine and was in his sixties. He walked up to Kevin and placed his hand on the young man's shoulder.

"Kevin I was moved by your prayer to the Lord. When I came in and heard you in conversation with the Father, I took a seat because I knew I was watching the Lord at work. I joined you. I prayed to the Father to grant you the clarity you were asking for. I knew I was watching a soul cleansed and changed. I'm sorry if I interrupted you. I didn't mean to eavesdrop on your moment with the Lord"

"Oh, no, it's cool, Pastor. I just wanted to see Richard before the service. I'm not really big on funerals and so I wanted slip in and say what I had to say. I really think I need to go home. I'm not feeling too well."

"No, you're going to be fine, Kevin. I don't want to be rude, but I want to let you know that God understands. He placed you where he placed you for His own reasons. You took a big step today, and I want to ask you to take another. I want you to give your testimony to everyone today during the service"

Kevin stared back perplexed.

"I understand why you would ask Pastor, but I don't think I would know what to do or say in front of all those people hating every word coming out of my mouth."

Pastor Ray patted Kevin on the back to reassure him. .

"Listen to me, son. I've known you since you were a child. You've never had a problem with finding the words to say. It's at these moments when a child of God is tested. The moments when fear says to you "running could be so easy an option" But what you have to do instead is reach inside yourself and grab hold of the person the Lord made you to be. He placed you in this situations for this moment right here. To be his mouth piece to others who need to find him through you and your experiences."

Kevin paced back and forth. Inside he knew it was the right thing to do. He looked over at Richard's body and a warm sensation filled his mind. He lowered his head as an internal tennis match was played inside of him. He felt the same way he did when he was about to teach his first class.

"Kevin, if you remember some time ago, I said to you one Sunday with your grandmother and mother, one day you're going to have a tremendous testimony because of the way that you lived your life. Do you remember what you said to me?"

"Yea Pastor, I remember. Richard never let me forget that. I looked you right in the face and said that stupid line I heard from the movie, Hoodlum. I said 'I stay out of God's house, and He stays out of mine.' I just thought it was real cool when I heard Lawrence Fishburne say it. So I rolled with that."

Pastor Ray moved the chair closer to the casket instead of pacing with Kevin.

"Do you remember what I said to you after that?" Kevin asked as he stopped pacing and smiled,

"Yes, I do. You said the same thing that my grandmother said. 'God is in everybody's house."

"Just like you are, son, with your carrying on with the ladies."

Pastor Ray looked at his watch and knew he had to move this along. .

"Kevin, son, I told you when the time came, God was going to charge you rent for all the places you've laid your hat. Well, this is that rent, son."

Kevin lowered his head.

"I understand that, Pastor, but did it have to cost so much?"

"Oh, yes, it does. Because if it didn't cost so much, there would be no transformation. So again, I'm going to ask you to do this. Not for me, for the Lord."

"What exactly to you want me to say Pastor?" .

The proud Pastor continues with a sense of excitement.

"I want you to tell your story and Richard's story. I want you to give your testimony today to Richard's family and friends, to your family, friends. I want you to explain to them what you're sorry about, the choice you just made with God and what you plan on doing from here."

"Pastor, you're crazy? How can I stand in front of Richard's family when I am the cause of Richard's death?"

Pastor Ray laughed with a strong sense of playfulness.

"I have learned over the years, my son, is that one of the ways to get people past a bad situation is to show them God is real. And I saw that stupid movie, that gangster movie you were talking about."

Kevin looked shocked. "Father, you watch gangster movies?" Kevin asked.

"Yes, sometimes pastors watch some things some would think they shouldn't. I always ask the Lord to forgive me if I think I watched something which was offensive to Him. But yes, I watched Hoodlum. The reason why I mentioned that is to bring your attention to the ending of the movie. It was the death of his cousin who he loved and who loved him which brought Bumpy Johnson into the church. He knew it was his behaviors which caused the situation for his cousin to be killed. Pastor said.

Kevin lowered his head as he shook his head in agreement.

"See, what you're going to start to learn son, is, the Lord takes pain and uses it to bring people back home to Him. This has always been your home. Your mother, your grandmother, and Richard's family call this building home because they know the Lord. We've all been here and we've been waiting on you. I could see the greatness in you years ago, but you were caught up in just being you, which a lot of us are."

As they walk back into the main sanctuary which was empty at the moment. Pastor Ray took a seat in the first pew and picked up the Bible, which lay next to him. Kevin sat down next to him to listen.

"Kevin you didn't heed the warnings and when you run through the stop signs...well, you know what happens, son. That's why I want you to step up today. I want you to be the Bumpy Johnson to the people who are going to be here grieving. Just open your heart and speak from that pain. Tell them what God is doing to you right now. Watch how God will show up and make it right."

He walked to the steps of the pulpit and checked the microphones. He looked down towards Kevin. Kevin's eyes locked in on every word of the preacher.

"Now you don't have to believe me, but I'm not going to stand here in the Father's house and tell you a lie just because I want you to do something. I'm asking because his children and his wife need to hear you right now. Richard was a standup guy. People had gotten used to Richard being there when they needed him, giving whatever was needed to them. I don't think Richard ever said no to anybody, and he never missed a Sunday. He also stood here on a particular Sunday and gave the whole church every detail about his history with drugs and guns"

Kevin smiled

"Tell me about it. I don't think that brother even saw a football game over the last 15 or 20 years." Kevin said while chuckling out loud.

Pastor Ray chuckled. "He's not the only one, son. Thank God for Direct TV. I was lost before that. Only replays for me.

"Okay Pastor how do I do this? What is the procedure? Kevin asked.

"Son, you stand up at here at this podium. You look down at Richard's family, his wife and his children, and you speak to them from your heart. Don't worry about what anybody else is thinking. Trust the Lord is going to stand here with you. He will place his arm on your shoulder and make it all right as everyone is listening to you. You're not going to be the lukewarm saint anymore."

"Lukewarm saint? Pastor, you're the second or third person to call me that."

"Didn't your grandmother teach you about the scriptures, when two or more say something, its confirmation? Can I ask who else called you that?"

"It was my grandmother and Richard."

Pastor Ray smiled softly and nodded.

"Richard told me I can't be lukewarm for the Lord."

"And he was right Kevin. Well, son, when the Lord takes the scales off your eyes, it's because, now, he wants you to see what He wants you to see.

"Welcome to the Body of Christ, Kevin."

About The Author

K. L. is a happily married father of seven, Teacher and former Dean of students for the New York City Department of Education over the past seventeen years.

K. L. is the co-founder of Bravin Publishing, LLC (est. 2010) along with his wife, Tiffany Braxton Belvin. Bravin is a literary service provider, with seventeen titles to date. Bravin Publishing assists authors who aspire to self-publish.

K. L. has published credits in poetry, education, fictional and non-fictional works of art. Over the years, K. L. has changed his style of writing from erotic and sexually based content to romance, spiritual inspirations and social promotion due to personal religious choices.

In 2007, he published his first book of poetry **"A Man in Transition"** which reflected his growth and personal transition. In 2011, K. L. penned his memoir, titled **"From Gigolo to Jesus"**, a book dedicated to helping others learn from K. L.'s torrid past. It was his hope to offer the world focused insight of a man who has completely transformed his life from one of misogyny to helping and supporting others. His writing proves his growth as a man, educator, and husband who attempts to offer counsel, entertainment, and guidance to all he meets.

K. L. has been fortunate enough to have performed and or appeared on various national and internet magazine and radio shows including Ebony Magazine, Black Expression Book Club, Hot 97 FM, New York; 98.7 KISS FM, New York; Urban Literary Review, Black Authors Network, The Beautiful Butterfly Show and many others.

K. L. has performed spoken word at New York's Bowery Poetry Club, Harlem Book Fair Long Island, Untamed Talent Presents, and various other poetic locations throughout New York City and surrounding areas.

K. L. possesses an A.A.S. in Business from Kingsborough Community College, City University of New York; a B.S. in Education from York College, City University of New York and a Master's degree in Education, from Walden University. In 2016, K. L. anticipates beginning his second Master's degree studies in Ministry and Counseling at Liberty University, Virginia. K. L. credits his enormous success to God and his wife who also serves as his best friend and business partner.

From Gigolo to Jesus

by

K. L. Belvin

Sex vs. Love

I didn't know what love was supposed to be between partners. The only love I had experienced was from my family, and because there was no male role model to show me how a man is supposed to act toward his mate, I was oblivious to the fact that there should be love in my relationships and in fact I should have chosen my relationships better. One of the things that a young man will come across in his life once he gives into his sexual nature is he will now have to deal with the emotions that come with sexual feelings. As a man, when you have chosen to connect sexually with different women, you have to deal with the different emotions that come with them.

The only preference I had when it came to women was they had to be full-figured. If you were smaller than a size fourteen, I wasn't looking at you, but other than that your appearance, education, financial status, career, neither physical nor mental impairments were obstacles for me. I didn't care how many children you had, if you had just came out of a messed up relationship, or if you were currently in one. I didn't even have to be physically attracted to you, in all honesty. Full-figured women who are thought to be less attractive were easier to manipulate because they weren't used to receiving attention.

I need to interject here that in addition to plus-sized women, I also had an affection for ghetto girls. The "ghetto girl" refers to women that come from low economic situations, and tend not to stray far from it. The saying is "You can take the girl out of the ghetto, but you can't take the ghetto out of the girl." When dealing with a ghetto girl, often, you'll deal with women that have lower expectations and aspirations for themselves. They become easier targets for sexual escapades because their self-esteem or self-worth may be limited or jaded. Once you understand how to pay them the attention needed, make them feel comfortable, then the opportunity to have sex is there. There are ghetto girls that feel, and in some cases, have been taught by the ghetto women that have raised them that it's their duty to have sex with you simply because you took them on a date or treated them nice. It's their way of showing their appreciation.

Prostitute, ghetto girl, or business woman, none of it mattered if you were not a plus-sized woman. Now, to clarify, I didn't target plus-sized women. My aesthetic preference is a plus-sized woman. However, I have to admit women of size are easy targets because they are constantly under attack by society. All I had to do was become something a little bit different than the norm and the doors were open. You could spot the insecurities right away. Giving well placed comments or taking note of something minute as the color of her nail polish could go further than you would believe. All of the things that women think matters didn't then and doesn't matter to men who are only looking to have sex because once your clothes come off, you are no different than that last chick they bedded.

On the inside, however, I wanted to have a girlfriend who I could care about, but I didn't understand why I even wanted it. I had a desire to be loved, not knowing it was love, while sex was clearly at the steering wheel. I always had someone I called my girlfriend while still trying to sleep with everyone else. When I was 18, I had a girlfriend that I met through a friend. She was the first woman I actually felt love for. Everything about her fascinated me. The way she spoke, walked, and smelled captivated me. It was something I'd never experienced before and even then I knew it was love. When we first met, we must have talked for about four hours then exchanged numbers. Later on that day, we talked for another couple of hours. So I knew this was different because all of my previous relationships began and ended with "When are we going to have sex?"

"Jill" and I began dating and instead of me listening to my mother's advice that I needed to be with one woman, I honestly believed there was nothing wrong with me having a girlfriend that I loved and treated well, but at the same time having other women that I used on occasion to have sex with. I didn't know that you weren't supposed to have other women when you had someone you were calling your "girlfriend." In my world, as long as I could keep the whorish man that I was separated from the man that I was trying to be with this young lady, then the world was good. I didn't apply any pressure to her to have sex: One, because I actually respected her and two, because I had other women to take care of me if I needed. I learned to be romantic and nurturing. The loving young man that my mother was trying to raise was slowly coming forth.

Jill and I had the typical boyfriend-girlfriend scenario. She came to my basketball games to cheer me on. She wore my school jacket. When I think back, God had blessed me with an equal because all of my weaknesses were her strengths. My callousness and ego were tempered by her humility and passion for life. She was a great singer and I loved to listen to her. Where her self-esteem was shaken, I had extra and I refused to allow any--one to speak negatively of her.

She took up more of my mind and time than I was used to any- -one woman having, but like Dr. Jekyll and Mr. Hyde, once I had hung up the phone, took her home, and she was no longer around, I became that other side of me. I evolved into a creature with two faces, and those faces switched back and forth when needed. This creature operated unabated for some time, but you can't live in New York City with a population of five to seven million people and not run into someone who knows you, knows of you, and or knows the current person you're dating. My ego allowed me to think I was greater than that.

As our relationship grew and we started to come upon the holi-days, Jill and I had agreed we were going to keep gift giving very simple. This was one of the greatest experiences, outside of sex, that I had ever had in a relationship. It was honestly the first. Jill gave me a stuffed toy Garfield cat because she knew I was a fan of the cartoon. When it was my turn to give a gift, I decided to do it at school. Anyone who knows me knows that even when I do something simple it has to be grandiose. We were sitting in the main lounge where all the students hung out waiting for their next class. On one side was a wall of windows from floor to ceiling. I could see when a friend of mine came out of her car with the gift I was giving Jill. It was a huge stuffed toy horse. I stepped outside and when I came back I was carrying this gigantic horse on my back. I crave attention so it was nothing for me to stand on a table in the middle of the lounge and explain to everyone that the stuffed animal was for my lovely girlfriend. I almost fell off the table, but everyone laughed.

A few hours later, I overheard her tell a girlfriend she wanted a Fendi pocketbook. I had no idea who or what Fendi was, but I could hear the excitement in her voice about having one. I was big on romantic statements, and I was going to try to do something special. Armed with grant money that was supposed to be for my tuition, I decided to get a Fendi bag for her for Christmas. I was told the place to get a Fendi bag was Macy's department store. The Christmas holiday in New York is not just happy greetings and good cheer. You have overcrowded streets, cranky pedestrians, and tempers pushed to the limits at times. It was bedlam, but I was determined to get a gift to impress my girlfriend.

When I walked into Macy's, I was immediately in a sea of bod-ies scurrying back and forth. It was like every movie you have seen of New York City, but multiply it by ten. Between the Christmas music, the noise, and the voices, it was easy to become overwhelmed, but I was powered by love. I was so focused that it was almost silent as I looked for a salesperson to help me find Fendi. Instead I found a neat and professionally dressed security guard standing to the side.

"Good evening, where can I find a Fendi bag?" I asked him. He pointed to a whole section that screamed Fendi and said, "Right over there, stupid." Wow, only in New York could a young man ask about a very expensive designer and be called stupid at the same time.

As I walked over to the Fendi section, a very friendly looking saleswoman was smiling at me. She was about in her late to mid thirties and I could tell that she'd been working at the store for a long time because as soon as I asked her about purchasing a bag for my girlfriend, her eyes immediately lit up and she went straight into her sales pitch. Pulling out each bag placing them on the counter explaining what they're used for and their different features. I started to become overwhelmed. Now, I could hear the noise of all the people around me. The holiday music was starting to sound deafening. I was feeling pressure because I didn't know which bag to choose. So, like the ghetto kid that I was I based my decision on how much money I had in my pocket

"Which of these bags can I get for two-hundred dollars?"

You would have thought that I had just spit the "B" word at her. The saleswomen turned pale. Her smile disappeared, and she looked as if she had been disrespected. She snatched all of the bags off the counter and started to put what looked like miniature versions of the same bags onto the counter. They didn't come with any speech. They didn't come with any elaborate sales technique like she had just done for those other bags. It was, "Here you go."

There were basically three bags. One looked like a mutant Tootsie Roll with a little tiny change purse. Another one looked like a gigantic cigarette case, and the last one looked like a long wallet. She gave me the prices of the Tootsie Roll and the bag with no handle which I found out later was a clutch. Now, of course, when you're young and in love, none of that matters. It's

Fendi and it was real Fendi. Even though I didn't know I could have gone out on the street and saw one of the street vendors who could have given me the knock-off version for maybe twenty-five dollars, but when you're in love, you do stupid things. This was my stupid thing. So, I went with the clutch. It was two-hundred forty dollars, but because the saleswoman just wanted to make the sale, she gave it to me for $200. I headed back to Jamaica, Queens with a smile on my face.

Jill was due to come to my house Christmas morning because we agreed I would go with her to her grandmother's house Christmas night. She had Christmas breakfast with my mother, sisters, and me. After we all settled down and got comfortable in the living room, I gave Jill her gift. We had already exchanged gifts, so she wasn't expecting anything else.

"What is this?"

This is where, when I look back at myself, I realize that the man I am now had roots in me then. The seeds were there, but the weeds of the sexual beast and creature that I was were so in control of my life that those seeds had to take refuge in the mud which was my soul only to come out when they knew they were safe. Watching her tear open the wrapping paper was similar to watching a holiday movie and the characters are right at that moment when they are going to get their wish from Santa Claus.

She opened the box with the clutch inside. She picked the clutch up, never taking her eyes off of it. I could see tears began to form in her eyes as her fingers slowly caressed it. There was complete silence as the tears now started to roll down her cheeks. When she looked up at me with those eyes, it didn't matter what I went through to get the bag. I had accomplished what I wanted and that was to send from my heart to her heart how I felt. Oh, I can still feel the hug and I can still feel the kiss and I can still feel that excitement of that moment.

Luke Warm Saint